SEDUCING THE FIREMAN

A RISKY BUSINESS NOVEL

JENNIFER BONDS

Seducing the Fireman

Cover Design by Jennifer Bonds
Cover Art from Deposit Photos
ISBN: 978-1-953794-38-3

www.jenniferbonds.com

To all the real-life heroes—thank you.

1

JAX

Jackson Hart had always wanted a brother. Now that he had a dozen? He was seriously reconsidering his position. He took a pull on his beer, letting the icy cold draft slide down his throat as he studied the rowdy, testosterone-fueled men encircling him.

They'd been riding him hard about being the new guy on the job, but that was expected.

Hell, it was nothing compared to his days as a probationary firefighter.

No, the only thing that mattered now was watching his step. The last thing he needed was a god-awful nickname he couldn't shake. And firefighters loved nicknames almost as much as they loved the job.

So, yeah, he'd have to make sure he didn't go and do something stupid that would haunt him for eternity.

Transferring into the company, he'd known it would be an uphill battle to gain their acceptance. Most of these men had worked side by side for years, and they didn't know him from Adam. As far as they were concerned, he was probably only a half step above a probie.

And that was only because he had actual experience.

It didn't matter. Given time, he'd prove himself. It wasn't like he had any other distractions. His sole focus was the job. It was all he had.

"Hey, pretty boy."

The muscles in his back tensed instinctively at the challenge.

Jax turned his head, finding O'Rourke staring straight at him, arms crossed over his puffed-out chest, a bottle of Brooklyn Lager dangling from his meaty fist. The kid smirked, looking pleased with himself. Too bad he'd lost points for originality. It wasn't the first time in his career the name had been thrown at him.

It wouldn't stick. He'd make sure of it.

Jax set his beer down and leaned forward, resting his elbows on the slick bar. All the guys were watching him now, waiting to see how he'd respond. This was the moment of truth. "Nobody prettier in this bar than you, O'Rourke. Just don't tell the ladies I said so."

The tips of O'Rourke's ears burned brighter than his hair, and the guys roared with laughter.

Anderson slapped him on the back. "Welcome to the family, Lieutenant."

Tipping his beer at O'Rourke, he signaled the kid there were no hard feelings.

After all, they were brothers now. By blood, sweat, and tears, if not by birth.

It was all he'd ever wanted. A family. A place to call home.

Growing up he'd never really had either. Brooklyn had come the closest. That was why he'd returned after years of bouncing from city to city. It was time to put down roots, something his own broken family had never provided.

Family.

What a joke. If it weren't for the Mancinis he wouldn't even know the meaning of the word.

Raised by a deadbeat father whose existence was predicated solely on staying one drunken step ahead of the bill collectors, Jax's childhood had been anything but stable. The two years he'd spent hanging out in the Mancinis' kitchen had been the best of his life.

They'd been a real family. Talking, laughing, and even correcting his non-existent table manners. They'd taken him in when his own father hadn't cared enough to make sure there was food on the table. He'd never let on how bad things were at home, or that the meals the Mancinis provided were often the only ones he'd eaten.

Ten years later, he still thought about them almost daily. He would never forget their kindness.

Or Frankie.

Just the thought of her had him grinning like a fool.

The little pink valentine she'd tucked into his backpack had seemed harmless enough at the time. He'd had no idea it would change his life when he tore open the flap. Or that the girl who gave it to him would haunt his dreams for years to come, her shy smile the last thing he thought about each night before drifting off to sleep. Which was why he had every intention of looking her up.

It was time to put the ghosts of the past to rest.

But first things first.

Priority one had to be getting settled, at the station and in his apartment. Twenty-six years of living like a rolling stone had taught him to live sparsely. There hadn't been much to bring from Boston, and if he planned to make a life for himself in New York, something permanent, he was going to need some essentials.

Like an actual bed.

Maybe some dishes. A real couch. The basics.

The prospect sent his blood pressure soaring. Shopping

scared him more than a five-alarm blaze, but if that was the price of stability, he'd gladly pay it.

After? Well, that was a different story, wasn't it? He'd moved back to the city for the job, but that didn't mean he couldn't see about a girl.

And he knew just the one.

He and Frankie had unfinished business.

2

BECCA

BECCA MANCINI WATCHED SILENTLY as Jax and his buddies celebrated, fist bumping one another and having a grand old boy's night out. When they'd first jostled their way up to Stout's seventy-five-foot bar, she hadn't paid much attention. After all, a bunch of Hulk-sized hockey fans were nothing to get excited about.

No, what grabbed her attention was a familiar face. One she hadn't seen in damn near ten years. One she never expected to see again, never *wanted* to see again.

Oh, he'd grown up and filled out, but it was him all right. She'd know those baby blues anywhere. Couldn't forget them if she tried.

After all, how many nights had she cried herself to sleep thinking about them?

Jackson-*freaking*-Hart.

One of the guys slapped him on the back and handed him a beer.

Figured. He was as popular with the men as he'd been with the ladies growing up.

Not that she was surprised. He'd always had a certain

charisma, that stupid Hart charm that drew people to him. Her included.

As a kid, she'd fallen for him hook, line, and sinker.

Stupid. Stupid. *Stupid.*

She'd been so naive to think he'd ever be interested in her. That naïveté had come back to bite her in the ass when he stood her up on their first date.

Talk about a wrecking ball. Her self-esteem had gone right to shit. But that was then and this was now.

Guys like him hit on her all the time. Not that they ever made it past three dates.

Yeah, she knew his type as surely as she knew her own name.

The familiar heat simmered in her belly, bubbling up from her gut with a thousand emotions she'd thought were long extinguished.

Would he even remember her if she went over there? Probably not. She'd grown up and filled out, too. There was nothing left of the scrawny kid she'd been. Gone were the knobby knees and the ridiculous crimped hair.

She cringed at the memory, taking a sip of her beer in a failed attempt to dull the ache in her chest.

No. Do not start feeling sorry for yourself. You are not that girl anymore.

New hair, new clothes, new attitude. Besides, her brother Christopher was still playing the field at the age of twenty-six. Jax was probably no different.

Odds were good he was the same self-centered douchebag who stood her up on her very first date.

And that just wouldn't do.

It was time Jackson Hart got a dose of his own medicine.

"You still with me?" Erin asked, twisting in her seat, trying to see who or what Becca was staring at. Her eyes narrowed, and Becca could practically see the investigative wheels turning. An up-and-coming journalist, Erin was too observant for her own good sometimes. "Or did you see someone more to your liking?"

"Hardly." Becca tore her gaze from Jax and raised a shoulder nonchalantly. Doing her best to downplay her interest, she scanned the last of the happy-hour crowd, noting the bar's cobblestone floor had disappeared under the crush of bodies pouring in from The Garden.

"Really?" Erin challenged, a sly grin spreading across her face. "Because it sure looks like you were eye-fucking those Rangers fans over there. Want me to go over with you? There are plenty to go around."

"It's not like that," Becca reiterated, fighting to keep the defensive tone from her voice. The last thing she needed was for Erin to march over there and blow her plan. She glanced at Erin's stilettos. The woman was fiercely loyal, and if she knew what Jax had done, it would take him a week to count the heel marks on his back. "I have an early start tomorrow, so I'm going to call it a night."

"You suck. You know that, right?" Erin's bottom lip jutted out, confirming she wasn't the least bit sympathetic to Becca's plight. "It's barely eleven."

"Which means it's almost midnight. I don't know about you, but I'd like to get home before the magic of the city wears off, and my carriage turns into a pumpkin." Becca fished through her bag and pulled out her wallet, slipping three twenty-dollar bills on the table. The other woman stared at her, curiosity etched on her face. "Drinks are on me tonight. It's the least I can do."

"Damn straight." Erin's pout gave way to a brilliant smile. She stood and smoothed her little black dress, and Becca followed suit. "Call me tomorrow, and I'll give you the deets on the calendar."

"Perfect," she agreed, pulling her friend close and giving her a tight squeeze. Erin had hooked her up with the opportunity of a lifetime shooting the FDNY Calendar of Heroes. Her PR job at Garden of Dreams was rewarding, and she loved giving back to the local community, but photojournalism was her true passion. If she played her cards rights, the calendar would give her the street cred she needed to get her burgeoning photography career off the ground. Working as a freelance photographer gave her flexibility, but it didn't pay the bills. *Yet.* "It's a long ride back to Brooklyn. I'm going to hit the ladies before I head out. No need to wait."

"Are you sure?" Erin asked, her brow creased with worry.

Guilt tugged at Becca. She hated lying to her best friend, but the truth was...*complicated.*

Shoving the guilt aside, she lied through her teeth.

"I'm good. Get out of here." She hugged her friend and slipped into the crowd, promising to say five Hail Marys when she got home. On second thought, better make it ten because she was up to no good tonight. No good at all.

When she was sure Erin was gone, she made a beeline for the bar.

You're Brooklyn strong. You've got this.

Smiling seductively, Becca squared her shoulders and sauntered over to where Jax was positioned near the end of the bar. She needed to remain focused, drawing on every last drop of confidence she possessed to avoid making a colossal ass of herself. In her haste to get this little revenge game started, she hadn't exactly taken the time to think through her plan.

Scanning the bar for empty seats, she quickly decided the direct approach was best. She really did have an early start in the morning and didn't want to spend all night screwing around with a guy who wasn't even man enough to make the ex-hole list.

Besides, revenge was a dish best served sizzling, and it was time to bring the heat.

Sidling up to the bar, Becca wedged herself between Jax and one of his cronies, which proved surprisingly easy. The men had parted like the Red Sea, no questions asked, when she smiled at them.

Suckers.

They probably wouldn't be so accommodating if they knew what she was up to.

If Jax was anything like his friends, this was going to be a cakewalk. He'd be eating from the palm of her hand in no time flat.

Hell, when it came to scoring a date, she might even clock a personal best.

Shaking the thought from her brain—because she would never go on a real date with this jerk—she studied her unwitting target. She was acutely aware of his body just inches from her own.

The guy really had filled out. He'd always been tall, but as a kid he'd been on the skinny side, always in a need of a good meal according to her mother.

Not anymore.

Much to her chagrin, his shoulders were broad and well-muscled, stretching his worn Rangers T-shirt to the limit as it hugged the taut muscles of his back.

She rolled her eyes.

Sure, he looked good enough to eat, but he was probably one of those lunkheads who spent endless hours at the gym and whose biggest fear in life was running out of protein powder.

It's now or never.

Solidifying her resolve, she reached out, resting her palm on his bicep—his rather massive, rocklike bicep—and proceeded to curse herself for noticing.

So not the point.

Just because he could wrap her in that steely embrace, didn't mean she wanted him to.

This was the same boy who'd broken her heart and left her crying into her pillow more nights than she cared to remember.

Looks changed, people didn't.

Jax shifted on his stool, turning his body toward her. He looked her up and down, his gaze lingering on the hand that rested on his arm. Their eyes met, and he smiled at her, a sexy grin that hooked up on the left playing across his full lips.

And, oh sweet Jesus. When he turned those dimples on her, her panties nearly went up in flames.

Damn. She'd forgotten those dimples. How was that even possible?

No matter. He was a player and she wasn't falling for it this time.

Fool me once.

"Can I help you?" he asked, the words smoother than a shot of Johnnie Walker Black.

Pretending to study him, she gave a coy smile in return. Then, tapping into her inner vixen, she stroked his bicep, relishing the way his muscles rippled at her touch. "That remains to be seen. I'm Becca."

"Jackson Hart," he said, offering his hand. First a smile and now a handshake? If she didn't know any better, she'd think he'd gone off and become a proper gentleman. With no choice but to accept his offer, she released his bicep and met him halfway, trying not to think about the way his calloused hand swallowed her own, wrapping it in warmth and sending a tingle racing up her arm. Or about the way her heartbeat accelerated at his touch. No way they had chemistry all these years later. No. Freaking. Way. "You can call me Jax."

"Because that's what all the ladies call you?" She leaned into his personal space, reminding herself it wasn't real. It was a set up. A role she played.

Jax needed a hefty dose of karma, and she fully intended to deliver. Nothing more.

"The ladies?" He raked a hand through his dirty blond hair. Interesting. Jackson Hart was nervous. She was sure of it. After all, how many times had she watched him do the very same thing as a kid? His hair was shorter now, cropped close on the sides with an artfully messy spike on top, but that gesture? It hadn't changed at all. "I just moved back to town. So, yeah, no ladies."

"No ladies *yet*," she said, correcting him with a growing level of confidence. Pressing her body against his, she snaked a hand up his arm. "Which means you're all mine."

"These guys might have something to say about that," he teased, hooking a thumb over his shoulder at his buddies.

"I'm really not interested in what they think." Licking her lips suggestively, she kept her eyes fixed on him, pretending he was the only man she had eyes for in the crowded bar. Men liked to feel important, too, right? And really, she didn't give a crap about his friends. They were definitely not part of the plan. "But I'll make this easy for you, Jax. Me and you. Saturday night. Eight o'clock. Co."

3

JAX

JAX STUDIED the sexy brunette who'd come right at him, asking him out without knowing a damn thing about him. They'd only talked for what, five minutes? Were all women in New York this forward? He'd had his fair share of dates in Boston, but no woman had ever approached him so brazenly.

It was kind of hot.

Fuck. It *was* hot.

Dressed in a thin white blouse and a tailored black leather jacket, she looked like she'd come from work. And while she'd come on strong, her confidence was a real turn on. He was intrigued to say the least.

But a date? When not twenty minutes ago he'd been thinking about Frankie?

It didn't feel right.

"Co.?" he asked, stalling for time to sort out his thoughts.

"Best pie in Manhattan," she said, arching her brow. "It's a few blocks over, on the corner of Ninth Avenue. You do like pizza, right?"

"Of course. What self-respecting New Yorker doesn't like

pizza?" He took a pull on his beer. "Best pizza in Manhattan, huh? I thought Grimaldi's held that title."

"Grimaldi's is good," Becca agreed with a smirk, totally at ease and exuding confidence. "If you don't mind waiting in line with all the tourists for a couple of hours."

A smile pulled at his lips. The woman had spirit. That was for damn sure. "It would give us a chance to get to know one another better."

"I know enough," she returned, her dark eyes shining with mischief. "For now."

"Oh, really?" he challenged. Why exactly had she come over here anyway? The bar was filled with men, so what had made her choose him? It wasn't unusual for women to chase guys on the job, but there was nothing to give away his profession, and this definitely wasn't the kind of place firefighters normally drank after a shift. "All right, then. Why don't you tell me what you think you know?"

"You're new in town, but you're a diehard Rangers fan, judging by the wear and tear on your T-shirt. You have good taste in pizza, you like a woman who can hold up her end of a conversation, and you were raised right, as evidenced by your impeccable manners." She moved in close, once again crowding him with her curvy body. How the hell was he supposed to think when she was so close he could inhale her perfume, a sweet musky scent that made him want to find out if she tasted as good as she smelled? "And strange women make you nervous."

She'd missed the mark with that last one.

"Actually, it's beautiful women that make me nervous." And she was beautiful. With long, dark waves spilling over her shoulders and eyes the color of bourbon, she had a wildness about her that called to him like a siren, begging to be tamed. The way her full lower lip curved when she smiled? It was torture. He could think of nothing but sucking on it, of tasting her. But looks would only carry them so far. She was smart, too. The more she talked, the more he wanted to take her up on that date. Guilt gnawed at his gut. "What gave it away?"

"Wouldn't you like to know?" She threw her head back and laughed, tempting him with the long line of her neck. His pulse thundered in response, and he shifted on his stool, his jeans growing tight. "Seriously, what fun would it be if I told you all my secrets?"

"Remind me to never play poker with you."

"I like to save the games for the second date," she assured him, squeezing his shoulder. "So, do we have a first date?"

That was the million-dollar question, wasn't it? The only thing stopping him was Frankie.

He scrubbed a hand over his face, questioning the likelihood of finding her single and interested.

After all, it had been ten years.

Ten years since he'd stood her up and left town without so much as an explanation.

Hell, she might not even remember him. The valentine she'd tucked in his bag had meant the world to him, but who knew if it had meant the same to her? And even if he did find Frankie, there was every possibility she wouldn't want to see him after what he'd done.

For all he knew, she was married with children, since he'd been too much of a chicken-shit to even call and explain things to her. But, really, what could he have said? He'd always tried to keep the Mancinis from knowing how bad his home life was. The last thing he wanted was their pity.

Which was exactly why he never imagined a nice girl like Frankie would give him the time of day back then.

So, yeah, there was a beautiful woman standing in front of

him right now, and they had off the charts chemistry. He'd be stupid not to explore it.

Besides, it was just one date. Pizza. Nothing fancy. Nothing long term.

What could it hurt?

"On one condition," he finally agreed, turning his stool so they were face to face, his knee pressed to her thigh. "Dinner's on me. I'm a bit old fashioned that way."

"It's a date then," Becca agreed, extending her hand palm up. "Let me see your phone. I'll put my number in just in case something comes up."

He handed her his phone, more than happy to take her number although nothing was going to stop him from showing up at Co. on Saturday night.

In fact, he was looking forward to spending more time with Becca.

They'd just met, but he felt as if he'd known her forever.

When she finished entering her number, she returned the phone. Their fingers brushed lightly, sending a jolt of electricity straight to his gut.

His cock stirred with interest.

Becca must've felt it, too.

She hesitated for a moment— as if making a snap decision —then she set his world on fire. Her lips descended upon him, gentle at first, but growing more demanding as they moved in unison—demanding and unapologetic. Not giving a damn who was watching, she crushed her lips to his, her tongue caressing his lower lip as she breathed new life into him.

When she finally pulled away, he was breathless.

Fucking. *Breathless.*

"Not that I'm complaining," he said, struggling to keep up with the sexy little temptress who had just rocked his world, inspiring a round of cheers from the guys. "But what the hell was that?"

"Consider it foreplay." Spinning on her heel, she winked at him over her shoulder and headed for the door. Apparently playtime was over. *For now.* She made it three steps before turning to face him again. "And, Jax? Don't be late on Saturday. I've never been very good at waiting."

4

JAX

JAX ARRIVED at Co. ten minutes before eight. In his line of work, it was always better to be early. And there was no way he was going to be late for his date with Becca. Not after that scorching kiss and her parting words. The last thing he wanted to do was leave that sexy little firecracker waiting.

Hell, it was just good manners.

It also gave him a chance to check the place out since he wasn't familiar with the Chelsea neighborhood.

Co. had a chill vibe, and he was always down for pizza, but communal dining? Not what he would have picked for their first date, since the idea was to talk and get to know one another, but the place was busy and the food looked good.

He checked in with the hostess, requesting a table for two, and stepped out front to wait for Becca.

As a kid he'd rarely travelled across the bridge to Manhattan, but lately he found himself doing it regularly.

Not that he minded.

It gave him a much-needed opportunity to familiarize himself with one of the other four boroughs.

A light spring breeze ruffled his hair, carrying the scent of freshly baked bread.

His stomach growled, reminding him he hadn't eaten since lunch. With the day off, he'd been busting his ass to get furniture and other basic essentials to make his place livable. Crashing at the station was fine, but there was something to be said for having a place to call his own, where he could leave the job behind and unwind.

He checked his watch. Eight o'clock and no sign of Becca.

She was probably just running late. No big deal, since their table wasn't ready anyway.

Funny thing was, despite his focus on reconnecting with Frankie and explaining things to her, he was really looking forward to seeing Becca again. And not just because of those soft lips, although he'd be more than happy to taste them again. With her quick wit and easy laughter, she was exactly the kind of woman he'd enjoy spending time with when he wasn't on the clock.

He loved the job, but it could take its toll—long hours, a shit ton of stress, and highs and lows that could wring a man ragged.

The trick, he'd been told, was finding balance.

Not that he could speak to it firsthand, since he had no family of his own to turn to when things got tough.

But somehow he managed. Always had, always would.

"Mr. Hart?"

Jax turned to find the petite hostess who'd taken his name.

"Your table is ready, sir." She glanced up and down the sidewalk. "Has the rest of your party arrived?"

He did a quick time check. Ten after eight. Still no Becca.

Shit. "Unfortunately, my date is running a few minutes late. Would it be possible to give the table to the next party and check back when another one becomes available?"

"Sure, no problem," she agreed with a practiced smile.

"Unfortunately, we can't seat you until everyone in your party is here, but we can keep you on the list."

"Thanks," he said, forcing a smile of his own.

Turning the corner, he pulled his cell phone from his pocket and called Becca. A few swipes later, the line was ringing, but there was no answer.

"Your call has been forwarded to an automated voice messaging system. The number you have called, two-one-two..." Jax sighed. *Voicemail.*

When the line beeped, he left a brief message and jammed the phone back in his pocket. It was too early to worry. She was probably just out of reach.

Of course, it seemed unlikely, given the entire city, including the subway, was wired. But she'd show. He was sure of it.

After the kiss they'd shared? How could she not?

Hell, he couldn't have stayed away if he tried. Whatever was simmering between them, it was burning red-hot.

Ten minutes. He'd give her ten more minutes, or until the next table became available, whichever came first.

Jax paced up and down the sidewalk, feeling more and more like an asshole with each minute that passed. Where the hell was Becca, and why hadn't she called?

He hoped she was okay.

When the hostess appeared again with a stack of menus and a tentative smile, his stomach dropped.

Becca wasn't coming. She'd played him.

And like a complete asshole, he'd let her.

5

———

JAX

THE NEXT COUPLE of days passed in a blur. Things at the station were quiet, and after working a forty-eight-hour shift, he was looking forward to a few days off. Getting blown off by Becca still chafed, but it wasn't the end of the world.

He barely knew her, and while he had no idea what had possessed her to ask him out and stand him up, it reinforced his need to make things right with Frankie.

Jax climbed the stairs at the station two at a time and joined the rest of the crew in the kitchen.

O'Rourke, the resident chef and shameless *Chopped* fanatic, was on duty, and something smelled damn good. The guys were gathered around the table, chanting "Chow, chow, chow," a sure sign dinner was running late and they were getting hungry.

"What are we eating?" he asked, taking a seat at the end of the table.

"Something special tonight," O'Rourke bragged, pulling a tray of marinated chicken breasts from the oven. "This little recipe is from Guy Fieri. It's got a kick that's gonna—"

"Turn up the radio!" Anderson called from the other end of the table, where his chair was tipped back against the window.

"This is some funny shit. These women give a fake number to creepy guys they meet at bars, and the station plays the messages on air. Can you imagine being one of these losers?"

No, he really couldn't.

Twisting in his seat, Jax turned up the volume on the docking station speaker.

Station rules were simple when it came to dinner. Everyone ate, and there was no television allowed, but the radio was fair game.

"All right, ladies, looks like we had a busy weekend on the Loser Line. It's days like this I'm glad I've got balls. I don't know how you all do it," said the smooth voice of the radio intern. There was a loud beep, and then the messages began to play.

Anderson was right. Some of them were downright tragic.

But one in particular captured his rapt attention—and the attention of everyone else gathered around the table.

"Hey, Becca. This is Jax. Jackson *beep*. We met at Stout the other night. Anyway, I'm here at Co. and it's about ten after eight. Not sure if I got the time wrong, but I thought we agreed to meet at eight. I'll hang around for another fifteen minutes or so, but if you get this message, hit me back. Hope to see you soon."

"Get the fuck out of town!" Anderson bellowed, slamming the legs of his chair down. "Was that you, Lieutenant?"

What. The. *Fuck.*

Jax's temper flared. His face burned, and he could feel the flush creeping down his neck as molten lava pumped through his veins. There was no denying it. It was pretty damn obvious it was him.

It was bad enough Becca had played him. Now it was on the fucking radio for the entire world to hear?

The situation had gone from bad to worse.

The guys were *never* going to let him live this down.

"Whoa! That's some coldhearted shit," O'Rourke said,

wiping his hands on his apron. "Did that chick from the bar really blow you off? That's too bad. She was smokin' hot."

"I don't want to talk about it," he said, clenching his fists so tight the skin over his knuckles turned white. "Ever."

Talk about utter humiliation. The guys would be busting his balls until the end of time.

"Looks like we got our very own Hartbreak Kid in the company!" McCoy chimed in. The guys roared with laughter.

Sonofabitch.

They'd found his nickname.

6

———

BECCA

BECCA WIPED down the bar at Mancini's, thankful for the Sunday afternoon rush. She didn't mind helping out her parents at the restaurant on the weekends, and the frenetic pace of the early dinner crowd allowed her to mute her guilty conscience, if only for a couple of hours.

Sort of.

She'd spent the last week trying to justify what she'd done to Jax, and try as she might, she couldn't stop thinking about that stupid kiss. Or how she'd stood him up on Saturday night.

What the hell had she been thinking?

It was so unlike her.

And that kiss. Sweet Jesus. She'd felt his lips on hers the rest of the night. Had fallen asleep thinking about them. Had found herself a sweaty, aroused mess as she thrashed around in bed, unable to get him out of her head as the throbbing between her legs intensified, demanding release.

It was a mistake. Pure and simple.

Okay, maybe not so pure. Or simple, for that matter. But kissing him? She hadn't meant to do that.

Impulse had taken over and, well, she just had to know what it was like. Just once.

And damn if it didn't live up to ten years of unfulfilled fantasies.

No, actually, it was better.

The real life Jax was all hard lines and sex appeal, something the sixteen-year-old kid she remembered couldn't touch. The way his tongue had mated with hers? There was no doubt the man knew how to take a woman and claim her as his own.

She sighed. Not the point. Jackson Hart wouldn't be claiming her.

Ever.

Too bad they still had the same old chemistry, which had shocked the hell out of her when their lips touched. If anything, it seemed to have intensified, burning hotter than it had when they were kids. And that ticked her off even more.

After all, how could she possibly be attracted to such an ass?

Clearly her ovaries were not a good judge of character.

To make matters worse, the radio station had actually aired his voicemail, kicking her Catholic guilt up to a whole new level of self-loathing.

Only, he had deserved it, hadn't he?

She groaned and dropped her rag in the sink.

It was time to focus on something else. Jackson Hart was not getting one more second of her time.

Besides, what was done was done. It wasn't like she'd ever see him again.

Erin would just have to find a new place for happy hour. No big deal.

Exactly. Ten years from now, the whole scene at Stout will be a distant memory...just like the broken date.

Grabbing an empty tray, she headed to the kitchen for more glasses.

Was it her imagination or were they going through more than usual?

She ran her eyes down the bar, noting that nearly every stool was filled, most of them with women.

Single women.

Single women who were no doubt there for the sole purpose of flirting with Christopher.

How many of them had he hooked up with? He was her brother, and she loved him dearly, but he was a manwhore if she'd ever seen one. At least the women knew the deal. It would be hard not to, since he made no secret of it.

Although she wasn't crazy about his lifestyle, she respected his honesty.

Given the choice between Heartbreak Hotel, population one, and the cold, hard truth, she'd take the latter any day of the week. There was nothing worse than getting swept up in romance only to be left out by the curb while your boyfriend—the one who said he'd always be there for you—eloped to Niagara Falls with his lab partner.

Sadly, getting stood up on her first date by her big brother's best friend wasn't even the worst of her craptastic luck with the male species. No, it was a just a fitting start to a dating history that would be almost comedic if it weren't her real life. She'd figured out a long time ago the Mancini men were the only men in her life who would stick.

And that was why she never went on more than three dates with the same guy.

Well, that and the fact that date number four inevitably ended in disaster.

Grabbing two trays of glasses from the dishwasher— there was no such thing as too many glasses when Christopher was at the bar—she shuffled back to the front, cursing her unused gym membership. Using her backside, she pushed the kitchen door open.

When she looked up, her stomach plummeted to the floor.

Jackson Hart was standing at the bar looking right at home.

Shit. Shit. *Shit.*

This could not be happening. But, yeah, it really was. There stood Jax, in all his god-like glory, with that strong jaw and sexy grin, giving Christopher a run for his money with the ladies.

Hastily swinging back around into the kitchen, she crashed into one of the servers, nearly dropping the trays in the process.

"Sorry," she muttered, keeping her head down as if Jax's x-ray vision could spot her through the swinging door.

She slid the trays onto a prep table and wiped her hands on the front of her apron.

In the ten years since he'd blown town, he hadn't called, emailed, or visited Christopher.

Hell, they weren't even Facebook friends. So what was Jax doing at Mancini's?

Only one way to find out.

She tiptoed up to the door and peeked through the window. He and Christopher were doing some weird dude handshake and chatting it up, apparently making up for lost time.

Men.

Christopher pointed to the kitchen, and she leaped away from the door, pressing her back to the wall and desperately hoping they hadn't seen her.

"Eh, Frankie!" he yelled. "Get your butt out here. You're never gonna believe who just moved back to the old neighborhood!"

Double damn.

Trapped. She was trapped. Her pulse thundered in her ears, drowning out the raucous sounds of the kitchen staff as they plated lasagnas and baked ziti and chicken scallopini.

There was nowhere to run. Nowhere to hide.

No.

That wasn't true.

Becca marched straight to the walk-in and locked herself inside. It was the only place to find privacy in the cozy restaurant. It was also the only soundproof place to vent.

Sucking in a deep, chilly breath, she let it rip, screaming out her frustration at the top of her lungs.

Much. Better.

When her throat had gone hoarse and her heart rate had settled from imminent cardiac arrest to what felt like a normal rhythm, she paced the tiny cooler, eyeballing the white chocolate parfait. Dessert made everything better. Maybe she could find the answer to her problems at the bottom of a nice Tiramisu cup.

Her hand reached for the sweet treat of its own volition before she yanked it back with a frustrated sigh.

No spoons in the cooler.

Besides, there wasn't time for dessert. She needed to figure this out.

Fast.

What was she going to do? It had become painfully obvious she hadn't thought this little revenge game all the way through. If she had, she might've thought to ask Jax where he was living, instead of just assuming it was Manhattan because he'd been drinking at a stupid bar near The Garden.

After all, she made the trip across the bridge five days a week herself.

One city. Five boroughs. Eight million people. What were the freaking odds?

Clearly they were stacked, and not in her favor.

The assumption that ten years of radio silence proved Jax's

time with her family meant less to him than it had to them? Yeah, apparently that one had missed the mark too.

You know what they say about assuming.

Giving herself a face palm, she leaned against the door of the walk-in, the cold metal sending a trail of goose bumps down her back.

There was only one option. She needed to own this. So she'd played Jax. It wasn't *that* big of a deal. It was certainly no worse than what he'd done to her.

No, it was time to stuff those guilty feelings down so deep they'd never see the light of day.

Straightening her spine and pulling herself up to her full height, she popped the door open and headed for the bar, a fake smile plastered on her face.

"Where you been, Frankie?" Christopher asked, throwing a towel over his shoulder. "Didn't you hear me calling you? Never mind. You're never gonna believe who's here. You remember Jackson?"

"How could I forget?" She crossed her arms over her *Speaks Fluent Sarcasm* T-shirt and turned a saccharine smile on the infamous Jackson Hart. "The real question is, can Jax say the same?"

Their eyes met, his growing wide as he realized Frankie and Becca were one and the same.

Guilt be damned. The look on his face was priceless. Too bad she didn't have her camera.

His jaw nearly hit the bar, but he snapped it shut before Christopher noticed.

The hurt in his eyes? Sure it stung, but if he was tasting even a fraction of what she'd felt those years ago, it was worth it.

Wasn't it?

"Be right back," Christopher said, eyeing a couple of girls taking seats at the other end of the bar.

Jax leaned forward, resting his powerful forearms on the bar. But damn if he didn't have that pained look in his eyes, the one that said all the things his mouth never would. She knew that well enough.

He was too proud. Always had been.

The Jax she knew would never ask for help, even when he needed it most.

"Well played, Frankie. Or should I call you Becca? You'll excuse me if I'm having a little trouble keeping up."

Francesca Rebecca Mancini.

The family had nicknamed her Frankie long before she could stop them, and when she'd enrolled at Brooklyn College, the first thing she'd done was reinvent herself, becoming Becca Mancini.

Of course, she'd quickly learned old habits die hard, when her family refused to call her Becca.

So she hadn't really lied when she'd introduced herself by that name.

She just hadn't told the whole truth.

"I'll tell you what," she said, digging deep and pulling out that careless attitude again. "Don't call me anything. In fact, don't call me at all. We're even now."

That was a lie. They could never be even. He'd decimated her self-esteem during the most fragile time of her life.

There was nothing he could say or do that would change it now.

"Even?" The incredulous look on his face was like a sucker punch to the gut. He grabbed her arm as she turned to walk away. "I came here to find you. To explain."

Pulling her arm free with a jerk, she placed her palms on the bar, leaning in close so no one else could hear the anger-fueled words she'd carried for ten long years. "What is there to explain, Jax? You. Stood. Me. Up. You know, I actually thought it would be different with us. That I wouldn't be just another girl you made out with in the park." Her lips trembled, the memory of her first heartbreak resurfacing with gut-wrenching poignancy. "Pretty stupid, right? I thought I was in love with you." *Crap*. She hadn't meant to say that. Open mouth, insert foot. "But apparently, after everything, I wasn't even worth a goddamned phone call."

"Frankie. Becca..." He raked a hand through his hair, raw emotion flashing in his eyes. "It wasn't like that. I wanted to take you out. Hell, it took me three months to work up the courage to ask you. If I'd known we were leaving, well, I—"

"Wouldn't have asked me out?"

"No." He looked her dead in the eye, and for a second, the rest of the world ceased to exist. "I wouldn't have risked hurting you like that."

She hated that she believed him.

This was the Jax she remembered. The one she'd fallen head over heels in love with.

Too bad it didn't change anything.

"When I got home from school, my dad had all our stuff packed." He frowned, an expression that, much to her irritation, happened to be just as sexy as his smile. "I never meant to hurt you. After we left, I just...I just didn't know what to say. I'm sorry."

He slipped his hand over the top of hers, gently caressing her wrist with his thumb. It was a slow, sensual act, and her stupid breath hitched in her throat, betraying the fact that she was as affected by him now as she was at fifteen. She stepped away from the bar, giving herself some much needed breathing room.

No way in hell was she going to let Jackson Hart back into her life.

She was older and more experienced now, and she knew to protect her heart—at all costs.

"Eh, Frankie!" Chris yelled, jerking her back to reality. "We're outta glasses. Grab a tray from the back, will ya?"

"I've got to get back to work." Turning on her heel, she stalked back to the kitchen where she'd left the trays, leaving him alone at the bar.

It was no less than he deserved. So why did she feel like such a jerk?

7

———

JAX

MIND REELING, Jax sat down at the Mancinis' table. Tucked in the back corner of the dimly lit restaurant, it hadn't changed much since his childhood, when he'd eaten every meal he could with their family. Even the red and white checked tablecloth was the same, reminding him of all the good times he'd shared with the Mancinis.

Hell, how many meals had he eaten at this table, pretending not to notice the way Becca blushed when their thighs brushed?

Lord help him, he'd tried to fight his attraction to her, telling himself there was no way they could ever work, that her parents would never approve, that Chris would kick his ass for violating Bro Code, but it was useless.

Once the idea had taken root in his brain, he'd been able to think of nothing but Becca.

Her laugh, her smile, the way she looked at him as if she saw something no one else could.

Taking the seat across from Chris, he tried to wrap his brain around the fact that Becca was Frankie, the same girl he'd spent the last ten years dreaming about. The same one he'd come to the restaurant to reconnect with. The same one that had played him.

The Frankie he knew was sweet and compassionate.

She never would have done something like that—something so spiteful—on purpose.

Then again, he couldn't fault her for it.

He'd hurt her. Taken the coward's way out like the selfish son of a bitch he was back then. Leaving the Mancinis was like being ripped from the only family he'd ever known. And if he'd called Frankie when they got settled upstate to say good-bye it would've been too real, too painful.

So instead he'd done nothing, telling himself a clean break was best for them all.

He'd fucked things up royally when he left. But he was back now, and one way or another, he was going to make it right. Despite what Becca said, it was clear they still had chemistry, and he had every intention of exploring it.

Starting now.

"What do you think you're doing?" Becca demanded, approaching the table with a healthy dose of hellfire and brimstone.

"Your parents invited me to stay for dinner." Jax smiled, ignoring the way she was glaring daggers at him.

He'd faced five-alarm fires, twenty-car pileups, and impossible rescue missions. A pissed off Brooklynite was nothing by comparison.

Besides, it was impossible to think about anything but the way those black jeans hugged her curves when she put her hands on her hips like that.

Tension poured off her like a smoke plume from an egress. "You've got to be fuc—"

"Eh," Mr. Mancini said, pointing at his only daughter. "You

kiss your mother with that mouth? Show a little respect, Frankie."

Mrs. Mancini made the sign of the cross.

Christopher shook his head and plopped a slice of lasagna on his plate.

Jax stood and pulled out Becca's chair.

"Sorry, Ma." Grudgingly, she came around the table and sat next to him, scooting the chair as close to the end of the tiny table as possible, stopping only when Mr. Mancini said grace.

Too bad the table was designed for a family of four. It had never been a problem when they were kids, but now there was little she could do to escape him. Whether she liked it or not, they'd be bumping elbows for the next hour.

The thought had his balls tightening.

Being this close to Becca, drowning in her scent, but unable to touch her?

He wasn't sure which of them had gotten the worse end of the deal.

"Thanks again for dinner, Mrs. Mancini." He smiled at the woman he'd once viewed as a surrogate mother. "I sure have missed your cooking. They don't make sauce like this in Boston."

Mrs. Mancini beamed at him. "You're welcome at our table anytime, Jackson. We still do dinner every Sunday. You join us whenever you can."

Becca choked on her water, spitting it across the table at her brother.

"Jesus, Frankie." Chris wiped his face with a napkin. "What's with you today?"

"Thank you, ma'am," he said, answering Mrs. Mancini. He glanced at Becca, who had fully recovered and was once again giving him the side eye. Good. He liked a woman with a little fire in her belly. "With my schedule, that could be a little tough, but I'll be taking you up on that offer every chance I get."

Becca gripped her fork so hard her knuckles turned whiter than the ceramic Deruta plate in front of her.

"What're you doing for work?" Chris asked, shoving a hunk of garlic bread into his mouth.

"I'm a New York City firefighter, if you can believe that. Ladder Company One-Three-Two, right here in Brooklyn."

"No, shit?" Chris held his gaze, as if seeing him in a new light, perhaps wondering just how much his friend had changed over the years. Finally, he nodded, a show of respect. "Good for you, man."

He shrugged. "It's an honor. The FDNY is the best in the world." He glanced at Becca, who was doing her best to ignore him. In fact, the woman was shoveling lasagna into her mouth like she couldn't get away from the crowded table fast enough.

"You're not going to be in that meat calendar Frankie's shooting, are you?" Chris smirked at his sister. "What's it called again?"

Becca's fork froze halfway to her mouth, her face turning the same robust shade of crimson as her mom's homemade sauce. "It's the FDNY Calendar of Heroes, and it's for a good cause."

Chris grunted and cut his eyes at his sister. Had she just kicked him under the table?

Just like old times.

Mr. Mancini shook his head and kept eating. Nothing came between the man and his dinner. Some things never changed.

Damn, it was good to be home. He'd missed the Mancinis something fierce.

Not just Becca, but the entire family.

"Moving. On." Becca shot her brother a warning look that suggested he'd have two bruised shins if he kept it up.

Becca was uncomfortable, was she? Time to turn up the heat. "We moved around a lot when I was a kid, but the best time of my life was here in Brooklyn. It's always been my dream to come home and put down roots. Been working toward it for the last ten years."

"Ah," Mrs. Mancini said, shaking her head. "You want to put down roots, you're going to need a nice girl to settle down with."

Jax grinned. Of course Mrs. Mancini would equate roots with marriage.

Not exactly what he had in mind, given the dangers of his job. The last thing he wanted to do was put someone he loved through that kind of hell, wondering day in and day out if he'd be home. *Or worse.*

It was the reason he didn't do relationships.

No, for the time being, he'd just be content with a little stability and maybe a home cooked meal every now and again.

Mrs. Mancini narrowed her eyes at her son. Like his sister, he'd mastered the art of ignoring the uncomfortable. "Not like my Christopher here. He goes with a different girl every week. What about you, Jackson? Have you met any nice girls since you've been back in the city?"

He turned to Becca, speaking directly to her, although it was her mother who'd asked the question.

She swallowed, the color draining from her face.

"Nice girls? Can't say that I have," he said, enjoying the way she shifted uncomfortably when their eyes met. He stretched, draping his arm over the back of her chair. "In fact, just last week, a woman in Manhattan asked me out and then stood me up."

"Can't imagine why," Becca grumbled, ripping a piece of bread from the loaf at the center of the table.

"Hush!" Mrs. Mancini admonished her daughter. She patted his hand, drawing a snort from Becca. "What you need is a nice Brooklyn girl."

"Ain't that the truth?" Christopher agreed wholeheartedly. "You just let me know when you're free, and I'll set you up. You can be my wingman, just like the old days. Plenty of nice, single women in this neighborhood who'd love to meet a firefighter, and who'd have enough class to actually show up."

Becca blew out a ragged breath, as if tamping down her fiery temper.

She was kind of cute when she was pissed off, but it was time to redirect the conversation. If this went much further, she was likely to blow.

And when she came undone, it wouldn't be like this. It would be in his arms.

"I appreciate the offer, but I've got my eye on a girl from the old neighborhood. I just have to convince her to give me a shot."

"Good luck with that." Shoving his arm from her chair, Becca stood, shaking that wild mane of curls over her shoulder as she looked down at him. "You're going to need it."

8

———

BECCA

BECCA CURSED HER SHIT LUCK—AND that stupid revenge scheme —as she glared at the man beside her. What had her parents been thinking when they'd made Jax promise to walk her back to her apartment? It was just a few blocks, and she was a grown-ass woman for crying out loud.

Would they ever accept her independence? She loved them dearly, but moments like this were exactly why she'd needed to get her own place.

She sighed. Unfortunately, she had bigger problems.

Like a walking, talking, infuriating firefighter who radiated sex.

Not that she was thinking about sex with Jax.

The man was trouble. Under all those "yes, ma'am's" and honorable notions he espoused, he was still the same old Jax.

And he was staring at her like she was the last slice of triple chocolate death cake on the dessert cart.

"You really don't have to do this, you know." Mancini's was half a block back and around the corner. They were officially out of range of her parents' well-intentioned eyes. "At the age of twenty-five, I'm perfectly capable of walking myself home."

"Sorry, shortie. A promise is a promise." Jax smirked and stuffed his hands in his pockets, drawing her eyes south, to a place she didn't dare think about. "Besides, you're only twenty-four."

Becca stilled, feet frozen to the ground.

Jax slowed, turning to face her, a playful smile on his lips. "What? You didn't think I'd forget your birthday, did you? You still have a few weeks to go. Don't be in such a hurry to grow up."

She rolled her eyes. He was two years older. It hardly made him her elder. Then again, Jax had grown up fast. She'd known it even as a kid.

He'd never talked about things at home, but she'd seen the way he flinched almost imperceptibly when her parents asked about his father. He hid it well, but there were rare moments when his pain shone through. No, he hadn't needed words back then. Those soulful eyes of his said it all.

And oh how she'd wanted to comfort him, to let him know he was loved.

Once, she'd come close to doing just that, hoping to get her very first kiss from Jackson Hart.

They'd been playing soccer in the small patch of grass behind the restaurant. Christopher had gone inside for a drink, leaving her alone with Jax. They were messing around, running drills like they'd done countless times before.

God, she remembered it like it was yesterday.

Jax was teasing her about being clumsy, and lo and behold, she'd proven him right, tripping over her own two feet, crashing into him and taking them both to the ground. He'd softened her landing with his body, and they'd had one of those swoon-worthy moments—the kind she'd seen in more rom-coms than she could count—where their eyes locked and her pulse thundered, drowning out rational thought. Common sense told her to get up, but she'd been frozen, secure in the protective embrace of the boy she wanted so desperately to see her. Then he'd brushed her hair back from her face, his gaze fixed on her lips. She'd been so sure he was going to kiss her...right up until Christopher returned.

Then he'd scrambled to put as much distance between them as possible.

It had been sort of sweet at the time.

Of course, back then she'd thought everything Jax did was sweet.

But that boy wasn't standing in front of her now. Before her stood a grown man whose eyes shone with confidence and pride, a man who knew what he wanted and wasn't afraid to go after it, judging by his words back at the restaurant.

He reached for her hand, but she dodged him.

Clinging to her independence, she took off down the street, leaving him nipping at her heels.

"And don't call me shortie. No one's called me that in...*years*." Ten to be exact, but who was counting? "In case you haven't noticed, I've grown about six inches." She shrugged. "Apparently Mancini women are late bloomers."

"You may have grown," he said, falling in step beside her, "but you'll always be a shortie next to me."

"Yeah, well, that's probably true of half the population of the borough." She looked him up and down. "In case you haven't noticed, you're kind of a giant."

When they reached her apartment building, he followed her up to the door.

"What do you think you're doing?" she asked, planting a hand on her hip and blocking the entrance with her other arm.

"Coming up for dessert." He held up the carryout bag her mother had given him on the way out the door. "Your mom packed tartufo for two. It's still your favorite, right?"

"Keep it." She crossed her arms over her chest. "I'm on a diet anyway."

"Liar. You're perfect just the way you are." His gaze slid over her body, assessing her from head to toe and giving her all the feels in her belly. It was clear he liked what he saw. Lust burned bright, flickering in those blue eyes like a flame greedy for oxygen. She squeezed her thighs tight, refusing to acknowledge her own desire. "Besides," he went on, "I don't have any spoons at my place, so if you don't invite me up, I'll just have to leave them both here with you."

Becca weighed her options.

Her mom's tartufo was the best in the borough, and if they stood around arguing about it much longer, there'd be nothing left but a soupy mess. Refusing to forgo a perfectly good dessert, she relented and opened the door for Jax to pass.

Once inside the apartment, she moved swiftly, making quick work of the carryout package. Then she and Jax settled in at the bar, spoons in hand. Only, the way he was looking at her spoke of an entirely different kind of hunger, one she refused to consider any further before dessert.

Instead, she dug into her ice cream.

"Oh, my God," she moaned, the dark chocolate coating her mouth with its silky goodness. "This is so good, I could orgasm right here."

Good one, Becca.

As soon as the words were out, she regretted them, but what could she do? He seemed to have that effect on her. Every time she was near him she felt like that bumbling kid again, fifteen and clueless.

Shit.

The last thing she needed was for Jax to think she had sex on the brain. Especially sex with him.

"Well, isn't that a sad state of affairs."

"Excuse me?" She dropped her spoon on the counter and shot him the haughtiest look she could muster. Who the hell did he think he was, anyway?

"I like dessert as much as the next guy, but if you think ice cream can make you come," he said, his words a smoky caress, "then you've never had a real orgasm. I'd be happy to correct that for you any time. Just say the word."

9

———

BECCA

SPEECHLESS. Jackson Hart had literally rendered her speechless with his nonchalant offer of an orgasm.

What could she say?

Nothing. That's what.

She was no blushing virgin, but the sexual encounters she'd had were nothing to write home about.

Not that she'd ever admit it to Jax.

Hell, she had a hard enough time admitting it to herself.

Grappling for something witty or snarky or just plain not-stupid to say, she sat there with her mouth gaping open. He hadn't even touched her, and yet somehow he'd managed to spark a fire in her belly, her skin growing warm under his appreciative gaze.

He smiled, a relaxed grin that made the corners of his eyes crinkle, and nodded at her mostly full bowl. "You better finish that before it melts."

How the hell did he do that? Offer her an orgasm and then just go back to normal conversation like he'd asked about the weather?

He'd done it on purpose. She was sure of it.

Because now there was only one thing on her mind, and it *wasn't* ice cream.

"I'm done." She pushed her bowl toward him, leaving the spoon on the counter. "I'm stuffed," she lied. "Couldn't eat another bite if I tried." Not the way he was looking at her.

"What? You're going to let it go to waste?" He grabbed the bowl, cupping it in his large hand, and raised his brow. "The girl I knew always had room for dessert."

"I'm not that girl anymore."

He rolled his eyes and took a bite of her tartufo, dragging the spoon over his lips before responding. "Sure you are. You can change your name, your hair, and even your clothes—I like the T-shirt by the way, very fitting—but I'll always know who you are underneath it all. Strip away the facade and you're the same sweet, passionate girl who used to pack me a to-go box after Sunday dinner, and who gave Sal Russo a black eye for calling her Frankenstein at the ninth-grade dance."

"You remember that?" she asked, covering her mouth to smother her laughter.

"How could I forget?" He smirked. "You made me give you dance lessons afterward. My toes were never the same again. Not that I'm complaining," he said, fixing her with a pointed stare that cut right down to her soul. "Sacrificing a few toes was a small price to pay if it meant I got to hold you in my arms."

She blushed—freaking blushed—at the compliment.

Shit. What was she doing?

Definitely not flirting. Not with Jax. Never with Jax.

After all this time, why was she still so affected by him? And how was it possible he still knew her so well?

He was too...*comfortable.* With her family, in her kitchen, eating her dessert no less.

"Russo had it coming," she said, twisting her hair absently

and doing her best to move the conversation back to safer territory.

"I don't doubt it." He took another bite of the tartufo. "Sure you don't want any more? Judging by the look on your face, you're fantasizing about this ice cream." He paused. "Or maybe you were fantasizing about that orgasm?"

Ding, ding, ding. Door number two.

Her face went up in flames. How did he manage to keep her completely off-balance, getting dangerously close and then backing off as if he could sense the ebb and flow of her emotions? He knew just where to push and how hard, without going too far.

She'd just have to keep her guard up.

"Frankly, I'm just trying to figure out where you put it all," she said, pointing to the nearly empty bowl. "By my count, you ate three slices of lasagna, a half a loaf of bread, and two desserts." She sighed. "That is so unfair. If I ate like that, I'd need a freight elevator just to get up to my apartment."

He shrugged. "I work out a lot."

That much was obvious. Heck, his muscles had muscles. And on Jax? It worked.

At least that's what her hormones seemed to think.

Then again, it had been ages since she'd had a man in her apartment, so maybe that's why her hormones were in a frenzy.

"Last bite," Jax said, extending the spoon so that it hovered between them. "Sure you don't want it?"

She eyed the last bite, her mouth watering. "Well, it *is* my dessert."

Finally, she leaned forward and opened her mouth as he maneuvered the spoon inside.

Her eyes drifted shut as she savored the rich flavors of the ice cream, and for a moment she was completely at peace.

Right up until Jax reached out and stroked her chin, just as he'd stroked her wrist at the restaurant.

Those fingers felt too damn good on her body.

"Oh, no you don't." She batted his hand away. "What do you think you're doing?"

Unfazed, he held up his pointer finger, revealing a smudge of dark chocolate. "You had ice cream on your chin."

Then, before she could even berate herself for being a slob, he put that finger in his mouth and sucked on it. And, sweet Jesus, if it wasn't the most erotic thing she'd ever seen. He sucked hard, sending a torrent of blood straight to her core.

"Sweet. Just like I knew you would be. Do you want a taste, Becca?"

Entranced and willing herself to *just say no*, she nodded yes as he offered the slick finger to her.

And then Jax's finger was tracing her mouth, exploring her with the promise of things to come. The man didn't fight fair. He knew her weakness—she'd always been a sucker for a good dessert—and clearly he wasn't above using it against her.

His seduction was slow, deliberate. He was teasing her. Testing her. *Challenging her.*

When she could take it no more, she sucked his finger into her mouth, taking him deep.

Jax wanted to torture her? To make a mockery of her pathetic love life? She'd show him.

Just because she'd never had a great orgasm didn't mean she didn't know how to give one, how to get a man excited. Jax wanted her. Had from the first time he laid eyes on her at Stout.

Ignoring the little voice in her head screaming *what the hell are you doing,* she massaged his finger with her tongue, circling the tip as he withdrew it from her mouth.

"You don't taste so bad yourself." Why did her words sound so breathy and porn-like? At least she was in good company. Jax's breath was coming hard and fast. Slipping from his stool, he positioned himself between her thighs, spreading them wide like it was the most natural thing in the world. It probably was, for him. Which was exactly why she needed to put a stop to this before it went too far. She needed to tell him to quit trying to seduce her. It wouldn't work anyway. The words were on the tip of her tongue when she blurted out, "I'm a much better dancer now."

Well, that was awkward. And so not what she meant to say.

"Really?" he challenged, pushing a loose strand of hair from her face and tucking it behind her ear. His fingers lingered, sending a shudder of anticipation down her spine. "You do realize such a bold statement is going to require a demonstration, right?"

"No, I—"

"Dance with me." Ignoring her protests, he grabbed her hand and pulled her to her feet, wrapping her in his warmth. Holding her close, he raised their joined hands and brushed a kiss across her knuckles as he began swaying in silence, his body moving in time to a melody that existed only in his head.

It was impossible to remember the last time she'd danced with a man, but that didn't mean she wanted to do it with Jax. Far from it. Dancing with Jax spelled trouble.

After all, wasn't this how it all started before?

If she was smart, she'd nip this thing in the bud. Stomp on his toes and send him packing.

But he was a good dance partner, and it was actually kind of...*nice.*

Following his lead, she gave herself over to the moment— it was just one harmless little dance—and enjoyed the press of his hard body against her own. His free hand slipped around her lower back, massaging the tired muscles and wearing down her defenses as he did magical things with those long fingers, kneading the tension from her with ease.

He pulled her closer, the hard ridge of his erection pressed to her belly. He was long and thick, and he wanted her. The knowledge must've short-circuited her brain because the next thing she knew, her hips were pressed to his, their dance taking on a far more seductive edge.

When she finally dared look up at him, she knew he meant to kiss her, knew she should stop it.

But she couldn't.

She couldn't walk away from that kiss any more than she could stop the Earth from orbiting the sun.

The pull was too great, her desire spiking as her body responded feverishly to his touch.

Stretching up on her toes, she met him halfway, their lips crashing together with barely restrained passion. Like before, his lips were soft against hers, both pliant and commanding, a stark contrast to the calloused hands that moved up her back and into her hair, twisting it without mercy as he drove the kiss deeper. His tongue skated across her lips, sending a very clear message about his intentions. When they finally pulled apart, her entire body was alive with sensation, a pleasant tingle circulating through her limbs.

"You're playing with fire, Becca. You have no idea how much restraint it's taking for me not to toss you over my shoulder and take you to bed." Jax paused, letting his words sink in. With his training, there wasn't a doubt in her mind he could—and would —do it. He caressed her cheek, his fingers blazing a trail down the front of her shirt, coming to rest at the hollow between her breasts. Her nipples hardened in response to his touch, her chest rising and falling slowly as her body screamed for more. "But I'm not going to do that. Not until you want me to. Because when I do? It's going to be the best damn orgasm of your life. I'm going to lick this lush little body of yours until I know every inch of it as intimately as I know my own, and I'm not going to stop until you know what it means to come undone with a real man."

"A real man?" Did he still think she was some silly girl, sitting around scribbling his name on her notebook? She wasn't that person. Not anymore. And it pissed her off that even now, he insisted on treating her like a kid, incapable of making the right choices for herself. What would it take to prove she'd changed? "I'm a big girl, Jax."

To drive the point home, she slipped a hand between them, cupping his balls and massaging them through the soft fabric of his jeans.

"Shortie." The word was barely a rasp. Their eyes locked. They were riding a fine line, one it wouldn't be easy to come back from, and they both knew it.

But dammit, she wanted this. Needed it.

The throbbing between her legs had reached a fever pitch, demanding she find out what it felt like to be licked from head to toe by a strong, sexy firefighter who was quite literally the man of her dreams.

So yeah, she was going for it.

She stroked the length of his erection, her breath catching in her throat

Jax had meant it when he'd said he was a real man, and she wanted every inch of that manhood buried inside her.

He captured her wrist, and one look at his eyes told her he was as close to coming unhinged as she was. "Are you sure you want to do this?"

"Less talking, more kissing," she ordered, snaking a hand around his neck and pressing her mouth to his.

She devoured his lips, enjoying the way they fit perfectly with her own. The hint of dark chocolate on his breath wasn't so bad either. Kissing Jax was everything her fifteen-year-old self had imagined it would be.

Sweet, passionate, toe-curling.

Moving his mouth over hers with precision and confidence, he seemed to know exactly how she needed to be kissed. And apparently he was determined to deliver, waking a hunger in her belly that had nothing to do with food and everything to do with the man in front of her.

Still, she needed...*more*.

Drawing his lower lip into her mouth, she sucked on it mercilessly, relishing the way his hands skated over her body, leaving a trail of electricity in their wake. If his touch felt this good over her clothes, she couldn't wait to feel those fingers on her bare flesh. Parting her lips, she granted him full access to her mouth, groaning when his tongue slid along her own, parrying as if they'd done this sensual dance a thousand times before.

The man was a jackass, but his tongue was heaven on earth. And she was ready to see what else he could do with it.

10

JAX

Jax held Becca close, inhaling her scent, a sweet berry blend that was probably a combination of shampoo and lotion. Whatever it was, it smelled like heaven. Still, he could hardly believe she'd gone from wanting to scratch his eyes out at dinner to lighting his fire like no other woman could.

How the hell had she downshifted so fast?

He didn't understand it, but he wasn't exactly complaining.

Kissing Becca was even better than he'd imagined. Her soft lips crashed against his own, her quiet moans urging him on as he lifted her up. When she wrapped her legs around his hips, locking her ankles and effectively closing the gap between their bodies, he knew there was no turning back.

Not that he wanted to.

He'd wanted her for as long as he could remember, and if she kept those punishing kisses coming, there would be no walking away...for either of them.

He slid his hands up her spine, stopping only when his fingers were good and tangled in her soft curls. Wrapping her hair around his fist, he tilted her head back, exposing her neck to him. A shudder ran through her as his lips brushed the sensitive flesh, his tongue forging a trail down her throat and over her collarbone. He licked further south, his free hand pushing her T-shirt up, exposing her breasts to him.

"Fucking perfect," he murmured, lowering his mouth to claim one of the buds beneath the silky pink bra.

And she *was* perfect. Curvy and soft, everything a woman should be.

"Umm, thanks."

Jax froze. Becca's eyes were squeezed tight, a sure sign she was giving herself a mental flogging.

Flogging? Now there was an idea for another day.

"Hey," he said, stroking her cheek.

When she finally dared to open her eyes, she took one look at him and lifted her chin, no doubt preparing to tell him off for some imagined slight. Before she could utter a word, he silenced her, pressing a gentle finger to her lips.

"If we're going to do this, we're going to do it right. No rushing. Where's your bedroom?"

She pointed and he carried her down the hall, enjoying the way her body curled into him.

When he laid her on the bed and she looked up at him with those big, pleading eyes, he nearly lost his mind.

"Tell me how you want it, Becca." He preferred to be in control, but tonight he'd give it up for Becca. Tonight was all about her pleasure. Because if she thought ice cream could give her an orgasm, it was clear there'd been no one to properly see to her needs, to explore her darkest desires. It was a fucking travesty. "Tell me what you need."

"I want you to make good on your promise." She chewed her bottom lip. "I want you to explore every inch of my body until I'm moaning with pleasure."

"Moaning?" He reached under her shirt, stroking the swell of her hip. "You'll be chanting my name. That's a promise."

She grabbed the front of his jeans and gave a tug, pulling him down on top of her.

Claiming her with his mouth, he pulled her shirt over her head and stripped away her bra with his free hand. He needed skin-to-skin contact, needed to feel the heat of her body pressed to his own. Next he went to work on her jeans.

When she moved to strip off her panties, a pair of tiny, pink lace underwear that didn't leave much to the imagination, he stopped her.

"The panties stay on."

She pouted, her bottom lip shooting out immediately.

"For now."

Without those panties, tiny as they were, he didn't trust himself to take it slow. He wanted her too damn bad, his cock begging for release.

Hell, he'd been dreaming of her for ten years.

Now that he finally had her? He intended to make the most of it.

Taking her hand in his, he brought her palm to his mouth and kissed it gently. Then he kissed his way down her inner arm, licking and sucking and teasing every inch of the way. She moaned when he moved on to her throat, nibbling his way down the curve of her neck. He massaged her breasts, and when he finally sucked one of those perfect little mounds into his mouth—*hard*—she cried out, her back arching off the bed.

With Becca under him, thrusting her hips against his hardened cock, it took every bit of discipline he had not to strip off his own clothes and take her.

But he was a man of his word.

Climbing to his knees, he settled between her thighs, massaging them as she watched. Lips swollen and parted, hair splayed around her like a halo, she looked like a fucking angel.

His angel.

"I'm still waiting for this life changing orgasm you promised." She was trying to keep the tone light, but her words were thick with lust. "The least you can do in the interim is take off your shirt."

Unable to deny her, he pulled his shirt over his head and tossed it on the floor.

Becca sucked in a sharp breath, her eyes growing dark with need as she studied the tribal flame tattoo that engulfed his right bicep and shoulder.

"See something you like?" The look on her face said it all, but he had to hear it aloud. Just like he had to feel her fingers moving over his body, exploring every inch of him with that feather light touch of hers.

"I've seen better."

"Really?" he challenged, pulling away. "Then you won't mind a change of scenery."

Without warning, he flipped her over onto her belly, so that her arms were extended above her head. He ran his finger along the edge of her panties, toying with the lace that hugged the curve of her perfect backside. She whimpered and wiggled her bottom.

He could relate. His balls were so tight they hurt. He wanted nothing more than to bury himself inside her.

"Patience." He gave her a light squeeze. "I'm not finished with you yet."

Moving down her body, he massaged her feet, then the backs of her calves. He lavished kisses on the backs of her knees, gliding up her smooth thighs and spreading them wide along the way. By the time he approached the vee between her legs, Becca was strung tighter than a clothesline.

She was practically writhing on the bed under him.

He pinned her legs down.

"If you want me to continue," he said, licking her inner

thigh. "You will not move again. You are going to lie still like a good girl and take what I give you, but you will not move again. Understood?" She nodded.

"Say it, Becca. Tell me you're going to lie still and take it like a good girl."

Turning her head, she looked over her shoulder at him, offering a coy smile. "Oh, I'm going to take it all, Jax. But I won't promise to be good. Not when being naughty feels so much better."

Jesus. He nearly came on the spot.

Becca Mancini wanted to get naughty? He *ached* to be inside this woman. His cock was rock hard, and if she kept talking like that, he wouldn't last long.

He blew out a breath, lowering his mouth to her thigh again. Testing her resolve, he licked the soft skin. When she didn't budge, he bit her. Nothing too hard, just a test, to see if she could take it.

She didn't move.

"Good girl." He kissed the same spot, soothing it with his tongue, and inched up her thigh, relishing the salty taste of her skin.

When he reached her panties, he licked her right up the center. Becca cried out, but didn't move.

He licked her again, this time applying more pressure, knowing it would drive her mad with lust.

"Oh my God," she screamed, twisting her fists in the comforter and biting down on the pillow.

"I thought you could take it?" He grasped the edge of her panties and pulled them down inch by inch.

"I can and I will," she bit out as he tossed her underwear to the floor.

Dragging a single finger down her spine, he admired the length of her body and cupped her rear, giving it a light squeeze.

She moaned and rolled onto her back, repositioning herself so they were face to face. A challenge sparked in her eyes, and she spread her knees, daring him to finish what he'd started.

Settling between her thighs again, he brought his mouth to that beautiful pussy and licked it, slowing this time to spread her with his tongue and savor the taste of her. He sucked on her clit, drawing her back off the bed as he massaged her with his tongue.

When he released her, she fell back on the mattress, knees shaking.

"That feels—"

Without warning, he thrust two fingers inside of her, determined to give her the pleasure she deserved, the pleasure that had so clearly been missing from her life.

"Oh, Jax."

Her body reacted instantly, gripping him tight as she rocked her hips beneath him. With his hands and mouth working in concert, he pushed her toward release, higher and higher as she reached the crescendo that would prove he knew her inside and out.

The way she had her eyes squeezed tight, biting her bottom lip? She was close. So close.

She just had to relax and let go.

Circling her clit with his tongue, he sucked hard. This time she cried out, her body wracked by a powerful orgasm that had her clutching the blankets as if they could ground her in the face of such intense pleasure.

When her body stilled, he kissed his way up her belly. Making his way back to her mouth, he kissed her slow and deep, enjoying the way her fingers snaked around his neck as she drew him closer.

"Sweet Jesus, Jax. I need you inside me. Now."

He wasn't about to argue. Not when she was panting his

name in desperation.

Her pleas had him off the bed and stripping.

He pulled a condom from his wallet and rolled it on as she braced her hands on the headboard, arching her back and lifting her ass for him. Climbing back into the bed, he plunged into her without hesitation, seating himself deep.

Becca cried out and he froze.

She was so fucking tight. Had he hurt her? Gone too fast?

He lowered his mouth and brushed a kiss across her shoulder.

"Oh my God." She repositioned her hands and rotated her hips in a circular motion, as if testing the feel of him inside of her. "I didn't know it could feel so good."

"We're just getting started, Becca." Slipping one hand around her waist, he found her clit, rubbing lazy circles with his finger as he slowly withdrew and pumped back into her. "And when we're done, you will never compare ice cream to orgasms again."

"*Yes,*" she breathed, as he drove into her over and over, pushing them both toward release with sinfully perfect rhythm.

It wasn't long before she was screaming his name, her body clenching him tight as she pulled him over the precipice with her, shattering like fine china and forever altering his reality.

Lying there spent, with Becca in his arms and his mind racing, he tried to put all the broken pieces back together. The woman had given him the best damn orgasm of his life. He'd known it would be good between them, but *fuck*. He'd never experienced anything like it before.

She'd ignited at his touch like a gasoline fire.

"That was amazing," he said, planting a kiss on her forehead as he climbed out of bed to dispose of the condom.

Grabbing his boxers from the floor, he headed for the bathroom.

"It kind of was, wasn't it?" She sighed and pulled the sheet over her breasts, stretching with feline grace.

"Yeah," he called from the bathroom. "We should do it again."

Jax slipped on his boxers and returned to the bedroom. Becca met him at the door, thrusting a pile of clothes into his arms.

"You have to go," she said, grabbing his elbow and steering him toward the door.

The *front* door.

"Hey, what's wrong?" *Shit*. She wasn't having regrets was she? The very idea made his skin crawl. "Talk to me, Becca."

"What's there to talk about?" she asked, giving him another panicky little shove toward the front door. "The sex was great, but that's all it was. Sex. It doesn't change anything between us."

She opened the door and gestured for him to step through it.

"What the fuck? Do you throw all your dates out naked?" he asked, temper flaring as he stomped into the hall. "Or just the ones who give you the best orgasms?"

Blood rushed to her cheeks, but she held her ground. "This wasn't a date. Good night, Jax."

Good night? Not likely. Maybe it had started off that way, but now he was standing half naked in a strange building, once again at Becca's mercy.

First the thing on the radio and now this? How many times did she need to humiliate him before she would accept his apology?

More importantly, how many times would he let her?

Stepping into his jeans, he promised himself this would be the last time Becca had the upper hand. He'd done her wrong, and she had every right to be upset about it, but no way in hell was she going to scare him off. If he wanted to get past her defenses, he'd just have to beat her at her own game.

11

———

BECCA

"QUIT HARASSING THE BABY FIREMAN, ERIN." Becca stole a quick glance at her friend between shots. The other woman was eyeing Mr. July like a cougar poised to strike. "That kid can't be a day over twenty."

"And yet he's so good with a hose," Erin mused, keeping her eyes fixed on the water that trickled down his face and neck. Then again, it probably wasn't his face she was interested in. "Seriously. He can turn that hose on me any day."

Clicking through Mr. July's shots, she studied the images with a critical eye. His patriotism was sure to set some panties on fire come Fourth of July. Really, it was a wonder she'd been able to keep it together with so many stacked firefighters running around half naked.

And if all those perfectly sculpted pecs and abs weren't tempting enough in their natural state, Erin had started rubbing the guys down with baby oil, leaving their muscles glistening under the bright lights.

She gave herself mental props for maintaining her composure in the face of so much hotness.

Too bad she couldn't say the same for Erin, who'd been in a perpetual state of lust all day.

The woman was on a mission to find out which of the models were single and ready to mingle—her exact words. Becca grinned. Only Erin could get away with something so absurdly cheesy and still draw men like bees to a honeycomb.

As long as Erin was focused on the guys, Becca could work in peace.

Win-win.

Erin had spent the morning obsessing over how hot the guys were and what a sweet gig it was for Becca. She wasn't wrong, but it was distracting to say the least. Especially with thoughts of Jax and the best sex ever dancing in her head.

Jax.

She could hardly wrap her brain around it.

She, Becca Mancini, had actually had sex—the dirty, erotic kind—with Jackson Hart.

It was everything she'd imagined it would be. It was also stupid. Like, unholy-demons-had-invadedher-body-and-made-her-sin-in-the-naughtiest-of-ways stupid.

What had she been thinking?

He was the only man who'd ever broken her heart, and she'd gone right ahead and served her body up to him on a silver platter. The moment he'd mentioned doing it again, she'd panicked. Big time. She still felt bad about throwing him out naked, but he'd warned her—told her right up front that she was playing with fire.

And like a hormonal teenager with no regard for the future, she'd rushed right in without a second thought for the messy consequences.

Well, no more. Sex with Jax had cleansed her system.

They'd acted on their physical attraction and it was time to move on.

No harm, no foul. No more third degree burns that would take years to heal.

She swiped the back of her hand across her forehead. Why was it so freaking hot? Must be the flames on the set, because it sure as hell wasn't thoughts of Jax raising her body temperature.

Becca shook her head to clear her thoughts.

He had no business being here today. She needed to remain focused.

After all, it was only the biggest shoot of her life. It had to go well. She couldn't afford any screw-ups.

The FDNY had taken a big risk entrusting an unknown with the annual fundraiser, and she would not let them down.

Hell, she wouldn't let herself down.

She had this. Because if she didn't?

Well, her parents' offer to move home was always open, as they were too happy to remind her every Sunday at dinner. But she wouldn't take them up on it. She was determined to stand on her own two feet, which was exactly why she'd gotten her own apartment in the first place.

If she had to work a day job until she got her photography business off the ground, so be it.

Keeping her attention focused on Mr. July, she snapped another half dozen shots as he flexed his ridiculous eight-pack and slung a coiled hose over his shoulder.

The damn thing probably weighed close to a hundred pounds and he was slinging it around like it was nothing.

It was totally badass.

From her position on the warehouse floor, she was getting a great angle on him, the light hitting his slick muscles just right.

"All right, Vic. Enough with the serious stuff," she said, climbing to her feet and dusting off the front of her oversize *I Love Wild Things* T-shirt. It was a futile effort. The warehouse was perfect for the shoot, allowing them to bring in charged hoses, trucks, and even flames in a controlled setting, but it was filthy and she was going to be a hot mess when it was over. "Give me a smile. A real one."

It was Vic's first shoot, and he'd been so nervous in the beginning, but she had some good shots of him once he'd relaxed. It hadn't taken long to figure out the guys weren't exactly on the job for the fame and fanfare.

Sure, they'd take off their shirts and strut around for a good cause, but they tended to be camera shy.

It was her job to make them feel as comfortable as possible.

The fans wanted to see them in their natural element, and while these guys liked to carry on and have a good time, they were all business on the job. Their lives depended on it.

Vic, bless his heart, tried to smile, but it came off like a grimace.

Time for a different approach.

She just hoped the FDNY didn't sue her for sexual harassment.

"Hey, Vic. Is it true firefighters go in when it's extremely hot and don't pull out until it's dripping wet?"

The god-awful pickup line earned her a real smile. He even tipped his head back, a hearty laugh rolling up from his belly.

Perfect. It was the shot she needed.

"Yeah, so don't prime the pump unless you want to squirt a little water," he shot back, shaking his head.

Becca laughed right along with him, thanking her lucky stars Erin had tagged along today. Her presence had turned out to be helpful after all, since she'd been quizzing the guys on pickup lines all day. The worse they were, the better she'd told them.

And they were all shooting for the stars.

She checked her camera one last time, ensuring she had

everything she needed from Vic. "That's a wrap. You're free to go. Nice work today."

The next few shoots went well, but when it came time for Mr. October, he was nowhere to be found.

"Have you seen Mr. October?" she asked Erin. If anyone would know if he'd checked in, it would be her. She'd even taken it upon herself to help with their makeup, smearing soot and grease on their bodies to get the most authentic shots possible. "Name's Johnson."

"Johnson?" Erin tilted her head thoughtfully. "Nope. Haven't seen any big Johnsons yet."

Becca rolled her eyes.

Great. They only had a few hours of natural light left. There was no time for delays.

Maybe she could rework the schedule.

She grabbed her planner, flipping through the pages with headshots of all the models and her notes on what poses and backdrops each would get. October was National Fire Prevention Month, so it was important to the FDNY. She'd just have to circle back on that one. If she adjusted the lights and the guys helped her—

The warehouse door banged shut, the sound reverberating through the cavernous space.

"Nice of you to join us," she muttered, shifting her attention to the newcomer who was strutting across the warehouse like he owned the place.

"He can check my smoke detector any day," Erin said, sidling up next to her. "If that's Johnson, he was well worth the wait."

"No," she replied, her blood pressure spiking. "That is Jackson Hart." *What the hell was he doing here?* She silently cursed Christopher for bringing up the shoot at dinner. The last thing she needed was Jax inserting himself in her life whenever he pleased. "Steer clear. He's trouble."

"You don't say?" Erin asked, checking him out with an appraising eye.

"This is a closed set," Becca called, turning her back on him and fixing her attention on her notebook. The words swam before her eyes, but at least she didn't have to face Jax.

"I'm your new Mr. October."

"What? Why?" She dropped her pen, blood roaring in her ears. No way was she shooting Jax. Without a shirt. Slathered up in whatever grease and soot and sexiness Erin could wipe all over him to make the ladies swoon. "Where's my Mr. October?"

"Something came up." He smirked, and damn if she didn't want to wipe that grin off his face. "You want a Mr. October, I'm it."

"You?" No. Freaking. Way.

"Unless you have another option?" he asked, widening his stance as if to challenge her. "You want to turn in a calendar without Mr. October, by all means, you're the photographer. But I don't think the FDNY will be real happy."

Stupid jerk had a point, but she'd eat hot coals before admitting it. "Fine. You want to be Mr. October so bad? Let's do this."

"Don't worry, shortie. I can handle it." He arched his brow and crossed his arms over his chest, sizing her up. "Are you sure you can?"

"Sugar, don't you worry about us. We're going to take good care of you," Erin promised, patting his arm demurely.

When she hooked her arm through his and led him over to the dressing area, Becca saw red.

Sucking in a deep breath, she willed her heart rate to slow.

So Jax was on her set. Big deal. She was a professional. And this was a paying job. She'd shoot whoever the FDNY sent, and she'd do it well.

Keep your enemies close and all that nonsense.

Busying herself with her camera, she tried— unsuccessfully —to block out the sounds of Jax and Erin cavorting not twenty feet away.

They were all adults. She didn't give a damn what he did. Although it would be nice if he didn't rub her face in it.

You know, since just days ago he'd been ravishing her body.

But whatever. It just reaffirmed her decision to end things before they got out of hand.

Once a player, always a player.

When Erin returned to her side, wiping her hands on a rag, Becca couldn't help but ask, "Having fun?"

Erin tossed the soiled rag on the worktable and shrugged. "He looked familiar. I was trying to figure out how I knew him." Becca froze. "Then I remembered. I saw him at Stout a few weeks back. You remember? The Rangers fans?"

Busted.

Damn Erin's investigative mind. The woman wrote a lot of human-interest pieces because she had a flair for the dramatic, but only a fool would assume it was due to lack of talent.

"So exactly how close did you get to Mr. October?" she asked, wiggling her eyebrows. "Please tell me you took a spin on his pole. That man is fine."

Flames shot up the back of her neck, burning her cheeks.

"Oh my God, you did!" Erin squealed. "How was it?"

"Shh! Keep it down," she pleaded, risking a glance at Jax, who was stepping into his turnout gear. The muscles in his back rippled when he tugged his boots, putting her body on full alert. "Amazing. But then I kicked him out." She paused. "Naked."

Erin's face went blank. The corner of her mouth quivered. "Kind of awkward he's here then, isn't it?"

"Not really helping, Erin."

"What did you expect?" she asked, completely matter-of-fact. "Mercury is in retrograde."

Becca narrowed her eyes at the other woman. This was no time for astrological mumbo jumbo.

"Don't look at me like that." Erin crossed her arms, taking a defiant stance. "Everyone knows pandemonium ensues when Mercury is in retrograde. Hell, I lost my keys yesterday and had to scale the fire escape like a ninja. Not sure what it says about my window locks that I can pop them with a credit card, but please tell me that man is going to make it past three dates?"

"Three dates? Not a chance," she scoffed, considering Jax's resourcefulness. How many strings had he pulled to be here today? It didn't matter. The three-date rule was there for a reason, not only to protect her heart, but also her sanity. She sucked at fourth dates. They always ended in disaster. *Always.* Like that time she'd made dinner for Matt and he'd gone into anaphylactic shock. Not exactly the best way to find out your date is allergic to peppers. No, fourth dates were bad luck, and she had more than enough of that in her life already. Besides, Jax wasn't even getting *one* date. "He'll be lucky to make it through today's shoot."

12

JAX

JAX FASTENED his pants and dropped the suspenders, leaving them dangling at his sides like Erin suggested. The pants hung low on his hips, revealing the cut of his abs, which she'd said would make the ladies crazy.

Assuming that included Becca, he was all in.

Hell, he was still fantasizing about her hands exploring his body, and he needed more time with her to make those fantasies a reality.

The photo shoot seemed like the perfect opportunity for face time. She'd have no choice but to talk to him.

Only the joke was on him.

Glancing around the warehouse, he took note of all the apparatus the guys had brought in.

He'd assumed she'd be shooting them in some small, intimate studio where he could exercise his powers of persuasion. Not once had he considered anything this elaborate, or a set with this many people milling about. He was way out of his league, but no way in hell would he admit it to Becca.

Besides, he had the easy job, right? Just flex and smile.

That's what the guys told him, anyway.

"Let's get this over with," Becca grumbled, waving for him to get on the makeshift set.

Tension rolled off her body like waves lapping at the Brighton Beach shoreline. He could think of a few ways to help her relax, if only she'd let him.

"Is this how you welcome all your models?" he asked, crowding her behind the camera as she fiddled with the tripod.

"Just the ones who insist on calling me 'shortie' and know dessert is my kryptonite," she returned, her tone light, as if she were smiling.

"What's wrong with dessert?" he asked, his lips brushing her ear. "I like a woman who's not afraid to eat dessert."

She sighed and lowered her face to the camera, peering through the lens. "You do understand this won't work unless you're in front of the camera, right?"

"But the view is so much better from back here."

That got her attention. She straightened her spine and turned to face him. "What are you doing here, Jax?"

"I figured it was the only way to talk to you. About the other night," he explained, hooking his thumbs in the waistband of his pants, doing his best to look at ease when he felt anything but. He hated being out of control, and being around Becca put him on edge. "You didn't really think we were done, did you?"

Smirking, she looked him up and down. "You mean after I sent your naked ass packing? Yeah, I really did. You're mistaken if you thought differently." She lifted her chin, the hard set of her jaw telling him everything he needed to know. Despite her nonchalant attitude, he was under her skin. "And crashing my set? Not cool."

"What?" He leaned in close, their cheeks nearly touching as he whispered in her ear. "Disappointed Mr. October couldn't make it? Sorry about that. But I'll tell you what— after the other night? After I licked that sweet little body of yours? The only man I want you thinking about is me."

She gasped, her breath coming hard and fast.

That was better. He needed her off balance, not lost in her head where everything was black and white, right or wrong. Better to set her on fire and have her careening out of control.

"My interest is strictly professional," she countered, cocking her hip.

"You haven't taken your eyes off me since I set foot in this warehouse, so you'll forgive me for saying it sure doesn't feel strictly professional. By the way, I think you've got a little something"—he rubbed his thumb across her chin as if wiping away drool—"right there."

"What I meant, you jackass, was how did you do it?" There it was, that wild look in her eye. "The models were selected months ago."

"Yeah, well, after that little stunt with the radio station, the guys in the company were happy to help me convince Mr. October to retire so I could take his spot."

"Lovely." She rolled her eyes, dismissing him. "We need to get started. We're burning daylight, and I haven't eaten all day. If you can rein in your ego and take a little direction, we should be able to get this done pretty quickly."

"When it comes to you and me," he said, tucking a loose strand of hair behind her ear, "I will *always* take my time."

13

———

BECCA

JAX THOUGHT he could strong-arm his way into her life? Well, they'd just see about that, wouldn't they? Maybe it was time the man had his ego knocked down a few pegs.

She glanced at her watch. They weren't *that* tight on time.

Then again, did she dare screw around on the job?

When he flashed her that panty-dropping grin of his, the one she was sure he'd used on scores of women, the one he probably thought would land him front and center in the calendar, the decision was easy.

"How do you want me?"

On your knees and begging.

Since that was unlikely to happen, she gave him a smile so sweet it practically sent her into sugar shock. "I'd like try something a little different for National Fire Prevention Month. You can go ahead and put your shirt back on."

"Are you serious? There is nothing okay about asking that man to put his shirt back on. Look at those lust handles!" Erin pointed at the cut of his hips. "Well, I guess I don't need to tell you."

"If you're not helping, you're in the way," Becca reminded her friend with a wicked grin. "Can you go grab Hot Dog from the back?"

When Erin grudgingly returned with the Dalmatian costume, she handed it off to Jax with a disclaimer. "I do this under extreme protest."

"What?" Becca asked, striving for innocence. "Hot Dog is the FDNY mascot. He's integral to fire safety education throughout the city. It's perfect for Mr. October."

Mr. November and Mr. December seemed to share her amusement, snickering at Jax's predicament.

"Anything for the FDNY." Jax slipped into the costume without protest, owning it like he did everything else. It was like the man had an endless supply of confidence. "Besides, women love dogs. I'll bet I get just as many likes as those studs over there."

"Sure, as long as you remember not to hump their legs," Becca returned, adjusting the lights. "Okay, let's get a few shots of you by the truck."

Much to her annoyance, he did everything she asked, no matter how ridiculous. And damn if he didn't look good doing it, which Erin was too happy to point out when she wasn't complaining about what a mistake it was to cover up such a fine specimen. The only time her friend expressed favor was when he got down on all fours.

Finally, Becca gave up, opting for a few traditional shots in his turnout gear.

They all knew she wasn't actually going to submit the pictures with Hot Dog anyway.

At her direction, Jax grabbed an ax and swung it over his shoulder, looking hotter than hell in the process. With the smoke machine blowing and the light sheen of sweat he'd developed wearing the fur suit, he'd be melting hearts all over the city.

With one notable exception.

"Try not to look so cocky," she instructed, adjusting her lens as he posed, the sculpted muscles of his pecs and delts drawing her eye as he swung the ax.

"I'm a FDNY firefighter. It kind of comes with the territory."

"Wow. That's deep. Do you actually need a hose to put out fires?" she asked, dropping her camera. "Because from where I'm standing your ego looks big enough to smother any flame it comes in contact with."

He flexed and continued goading her. "Don't judge a book by its cover."

"What cover?" She snorted. "You're parading around here half naked like Chippendale's finest."

"Damn straight!" Erin chimed in with a giggle.

Becca shot her a dark look.

"Just doing my duty." Jax winked at her and climbed up the truck's ladder. Strutting around bare-chested and sweaty, he was to-die-for scrumptious against the backdrop of a flame wall. Talk about unfair. "Seriously, though. You do know this calendar is about more than twelve months of hot firefighters, right? The proceeds will fund fire education and safety programs, as well as provide assistance to families in need."

Ignoring him, Becca snapped away on her camera.

She just needed to get the shot. No matter what she said or did, he was going to look good, and it was her reputation on the line. Why did the man have to be so damn sexy? Or self-assured, for that matter? He was infuriating. And of course the stupid camera loved him.

As far as she could tell, Jax didn't have a bad side.

Which was ridiculous, because everyone had a bad side.

Everyone.

Except Jax, apparently.

Her stomach growled, reminding her that she was starving. Exhausted, too.

It had been a long day, and all she wanted to do was go home and take a long soak in the tub after eating the biggest, greasiest burger she could get her hands on.

She'd grab takeout on the way home.

Judging by her stained T-shirt, there was no way she could actually eat-in. Not unless she wanted to risk looking like a vagrant, anyway.

Maybe hunger was screwing with her judgment, too, because once again she was wrestling feelings of guilt over what she'd done to Jax. She had to give him credit, though. The man did not give up.

Still, he was just the sort of here today, gone tomorrow guy she hated.

Despite everything he'd done to convince her otherwise, she knew what kind of man he really was. Didn't she?

14

——————

JAX

JAX GRABBED his carryout order and made the short drive back to the warehouse. He still wanted to talk to Becca, and if burgers couldn't entice her to give him ten minutes of her time, nothing would. The woman was stubborn as hell.

What she didn't understand—yet—was that no matter what she did to put distance between them, he wouldn't give up.

It wasn't in his nature. It was one of the things that made him so good at his job.

And with the fire blazing between them?

It was just a matter of time until she came around.

The set was dark when he returned, and most of the crew had left. Erin passed him on her way out the door, eyeing the carryout bag.

"Good luck." She grinned, not the least bit sympathetic. "You're going to need it."

At least he hadn't missed Becca. That was a good start.

Dropping the bag on the table, he went to work cleaning up some of her supplies. He knew better than to touch her equipment, but anything non-mechanical felt like fair game. Wherever she was, she'd be back eventually.

He just hoped she'd bring her appetite.

"What do you think you're doing?" she demanded, the heels of her boots clicking on the cement as she crossed the open space, stopping when she reached the table. She sniffed the air. "What's that smell?

"Burgers. I brought dinner. I thought we could talk."

She eyed the Shake Shack carryout bag. "I'm not hungry."

Her stomach growled.

"Liar."

Crossing her arms, she tried another obvious lie. "Okay, fine. I'm hungry, but I have no interest in talking."

"Suit yourself. That just means there's more for me." He opened the bag and pulled out a burger. Tearing back the white wrapper, he took a big bite and groaned. "Now, this is a cheeseburger. They don't make them like this in Boston. You sure you don't want one?"

Sighing, Becca put her hand out for a burger. "Fine. But no talking. I'm too tired to think. It's been a long day."

He fished her burger and two shakes from the bag, leaving the fries for last.

"When did you get into photography?" he asked, curious to know more about her passion. "I didn't know you had an interest."

She bit into the burger, chewing it thoroughly and taking her time to respond. "There are a lot of things you don't know about me. Time and distance will do that."

Walked right into that one, hadn't he?

Perhaps he just hadn't asked the right question. "Is it a hobby or is it something you aspire to do full-time?"

"I picked up my first camera at fifteen," she said, staring at him pointedly. Meaning after he left town. Maybe something good had come of his departure after all—not that he'd be stupid enough to voice that thought. "Haven't put it down since.

I've got degrees in Communication and in Fine Arts from Brooklyn College, but it's much easier to find a desk job than it is to make it as a photojournalist." She shrugged. "I'll get there eventually. The calendar is a great stepping-stone to get my work out there. Until then, I'll enjoy my time at Garden of Dreams and take freelance jobs when I can get them."

"I'd love to take a look at your work sometime."

He meant it. Listening to her talk about her aspirations, he had no doubt Becca poured her heart and soul into her photography.

Maybe it would give him a better understanding of the woman she'd become. Each moment he spent with her made it clear she'd grown to be a very different woman than the one he'd imagined, and as it turned out, he liked this one a hell of a lot better.

They finished their sandwiches in silence, picking at the fries until they were cold and the shakes were gone. Jax collected the wrappers and stuffed them in the bag.

"Thanks for dinner." Becca appraised him, perhaps surprised they'd been able to get through a meal—even a quick one—without the conversation disintegrating into World War III.

"You're welcome. We should do it again sometime." He grinned, unable to resist busting her balls just a little. "I hear there's a great place over in Chelsea that serves the best pie in Manhattan."

She stuck her tongue out at him. "Smart-ass."

"Give me your keys. I'll carry this stuff out to your car while you finish packing up your camera," he offered, grabbing the tower of boxes from the table.

He carried the boxes to her car, locking them in the trunk before returning to find the warehouse empty.

The camera bag was packed, but its owner was nowhere to be found.

"Becca?"

Where had she gone now? Night was falling fast, casting long shadows across the cement floor.

It was creepy as hell.

Time to find Becca and get out.

He made his way back the hall she'd come from earlier, calling her name to avoid scaring the shit out of her.

When he finally found her in a supply closet, she was bent over with her rear in the air, her dark leggings showcasing the perfection of her ass. Not quite what he was expecting, but damn if his cock didn't swell at the sight. The mental picture of taking her from behind was front and center in his brain as he watched her, eyes glued to her backside.

"Stop staring at my ass," she said, twisting to confirm her suspicions, "and help me find my phone. I thought I left it on the shelf in here, but I can't find it. Maybe it fell on the floor?"

She continued to rummage through the boxes and bins on the lower shelves, so he joined her, using his own phone to brighten the dim room as he looked under the rusty shelves. Crawling around in a dirty supply room wasn't exactly how he imagined spending an evening with the sexy woman beside him, but better him crawling around on the floor than her. Spotting a dark lump beneath the shelving unit, he reached under, hoping like hell he wasn't about to catch a case of lockjaw for his trouble, and pulled out the phone.

"Got it."

When he turned to stand, he found Becca right behind him. They collided, his face going straight to her pussy as her hands tangled in his hair, holding him tight.

They both froze.

The sexual tension in the room was so damn thick they'd need the Jaws of Life to cut through it.

Fuck it.

He gripped her ass, cupping those round cheeks and using them as leverage to pull her close.

She remained silent, as if waiting to see what he'd do next.

Keeping their bodies flush, he climbed to his feet slowly, savoring the feel of her soft curves against his chest. Their eyes met, and damn if he didn't want to lose himself in those dark depths. The way she was looking at him, like he was the answer to a prayer she'd never voiced aloud?

It nearly stripped him of his restraint.

A lesser part of his brain told him to take it slow—the last thing he wanted to do was spook her—but he ignored it, letting instinct take over.

Their attraction? It wasn't cerebral. It was primal.

"Don't even think about it," she warned, making no move to separate their bodies, although they stood so close he could feel the rise and fall of her breasts with each breath.

"I have no idea what you're talking about."

"You know *exactly* what I'm talking about." She rolled her eyes and shifted her weight. Was it wishful thinking or had she actually gotten closer? "Don't be coy."

"Are you seriously going to pretend you don't feel that?" He smirked. "The sexual tension in this closet is so thick we're both drowning in it."

"I have no idea what you're talking about."

"Now who's being coy? One word, Becca." He paused. "*Yes.* That's all you have to say."

Becca lifted her chin and licked her lips, leveling him with a look that said she was ready for the stare-down of the ages.

Figured. No matter how bad they both wanted it, she'd dig in her heels just to spite him.

She was so damn sexy when she was being obstinate, which only reinforced the fact that he was going to need a cold shower when he got home.

A mischievous smile tugged at the corner of her mouth, tempting him with every dark fantasy those lips had ever inspired.

"*Yes.*"

It was all the invitation he needed.

Claiming her mouth with his own, he lavished kisses upon those full lips, tracing her mouth with his tongue and slipping past the entrance to explore her more fully. She moaned quietly, her body melting against him as she began to tease him with short strokes of her tongue. Like before, that small spark of passion burned hot, growing exponentially as she raked her fingers through his hair and over the muscles of his shoulders.

It wasn't enough. With Becca, he wondered if it would ever be enough.

Hell, they didn't need words. Just touch.

As long as they could explore one another and lose themselves in the moment, it would be enough.

Spinning her around, he pressed her back to the metal rack, sending odds and ends clattering to the floor. Ignoring the mess, he slid his hands up her back, holding her tight as he worked his way down her chin and along the curve of her neck, licking and sucking and memorizing her heavenly taste.

Despite the long day on the set and the smudges of oil and dirt and soot on her clothes, her skin remained just as he remembered, sweet and tantalizing, like a drug.

Pushing her T-shirt up, he dropped to his knees, licking the stretch of skin from her belly button to her breasts, noting the goose bumps that raced across her flesh. He rubbed his palms over the tiny bumps, warming her with his touch. Looking up at her, at the way her eyelids drooped as she gave herself over to pleasure, he knew it was time to find out just how thick those leggings were.

She'd had a long day and she deserved nothing more than a moment of unbridled pleasure, something he was more than happy to provide, if she'd let him. Bringing his mouth to the place where her legs joined, he sucked on her clit through the thin material.

The whimper that followed was music to his hears.

Bringing his left hand around, he used his fingers to massage her in concert with his tongue, growing frustrated by the fabric separating them. She was mewling with satisfaction, hips rocking, but he needed more. Needed to touch that slick heat of hers, to taste it, to fill it completely.

"Take your pants off, Becca."

She hesitated.

Dropping his chin to his chest, he rested his forehead against her belly.

He was out of control. Taking her in a place like this? What the hell was he thinking?

She deserved better than a romp in the backroom of some sketchy warehouse.

Her hips shifted.

"What are you doing?" he asked, looking up at her.

"Isn't it obvious?" she asked, her words heavy with need. "I'm taking off my pants."

All right then. He wasn't about to deny her. Not now, not ever.

Jax climbed to his feet and fused his mouth with Becca's. She opened herself to him immediately, her tongue skating over his as she wiggled her leggings down to her knees.

"Good enough," Jax told her, dropping a hand to her sweet spot. She was hot, slick, and ready. Without warning, he plunged two fingers into her wet heat, earning a moan that told him she liked it very much. His cock throbbed with his own need, but he'd take care of that later. This moment was about pleasuring Becca. "That's right. Tell me what you like so I can make it good for you every time. I want to know what gets you hot so I can make you come for me."

"*Jax.*" His name was a breath on her lips as he pumped his fingers deep inside of her, hooking them forward and angling for the spot that would give her the most intense orgasm.

He rolled his thumb over her clit, applying more pressure as she rocked her hips against him.

"Do you like it when I fuck you with my fingers?"

"*Yes,*" she panted, grasping his shoulder for support, or maybe just to ground herself in the moment. "Don't. Stop."

She was close, spiraling toward release.

With her head thrown back and lips parted, she was the wild beauty of his dreams, the one he knew would only let go like this for him. Her body clenched him tight as the shockwaves of pleasure rocked her to the core. She arched her back into him, holding on as if he were the last shred of sanity in a world gone mad.

And in the dark warehouse, her moans of ecstasy carried through the night with complete abandon.

Jax kissed the top of her head as he withdrew and helped her adjust her pants.

Despite the orgasm that had just rocked her body, she looked at him with uncertainty, once again retreating from him. "We should go."

Once Becca was situated in her car, with her cell phone, he tapped on the window.

She rolled it down, looking apprehensive. "Thanks again for dinner...and everything else."

He reached out, stroking her cheek and loving the way she melted at his touch. "I told you, it was my pleasure."

She leaned her head back against the headrest, eyes closed.

The day had taken its toll. Even after their little tryst in the back room, she looked exhausted.

"What we did...it has to stop." She sighed. "We can't do this again. It's not...right."

Biting his tongue, he swallowed a snarky reply that would just start another argument. Why she insisted on fighting this thing between them was beyond him, when it was clear they had more chemistry than the periodic table.

"Drive carefully." He kissed her lightly, catching her off guard. Her eyes shot open. "I'll see you Saturday."

"Saturday?" Her brow wrinkled in concentration. A frown tugged at the corners of her mouth. "All right. I'll bite. What's Saturday?"

"Didn't Chris tell you?" He grinned and stepped back from the car, seeking a safe distance, outside her striking zone. "I'm joining Mancini's softball team."

Becca slammed her fist on the steering wheel and punched the button to close the window.

It rose slowly, not nearly quick enough to prevent him from hearing the string of four-letter words that would have her doing penance from now until the end of time. He waved as she backed out of the parking lot, enjoying his hard-won victory. Because if he knew only one thing about Becca Mancini, it was that she was going to make him pay on Saturday.

15

––––––––––

BECCA

BECCA LACED UP HER CLEATS, cursing Jax and his pushy, meddling ways for the eight thousandth time.

After letting him give her another sinfully good O at the photo shoot, the last thing she wanted to do was face him on the bench. She'd played every card she had in an attempt to back out of the game, but Christopher wasn't having any of it. He'd even cut her off before she could try the old "remember when" guilt trip, which was usually her ace in the hole and reserved for the direst of situations.

That was the problem with siblings.

They always knew your angle and which buttons to push in order to get their own way.

As the team captain, he'd guilted the shit out of her, reminding her the team was required to have three women in the rotation to avoid a forfeit. Then, to make sure she wasn't a no show, he'd piled on with an endless diatribe about the team standings. For the first time ever, Mancini's was undefeated.

So, yeah, while she wanted to be anywhere but on the field today, here she was.

Maybe she'd get lucky and Jax wouldn't show.

Fat chance. Like hell he'd miss an opportunity to torture you.

Slinging her bag over her shoulder, she slammed the car door. Jax would be there. No doubt about it.

The real question was why had she let him get in her pants again?

The sex wasn't that good.

Denial much?

Fine. The more likely answer was that she was clearly a glutton for punishment. Because no matter how good the man made her feel *right now*, there was only one way it could end. A fact she needed to remember if she didn't want him to break her heart again. He wasn't in it for the long haul, and soon enough he'd move on.

Figuratively and literally. The fourth date jinx. It happened every time.

She just wasn't built for relationships.

Dropping her bag in the dugout, she jogged to the outfield where the team was warming up.

Making a point of avoiding Jax, she settled into the grass as far from him as possible and pulled up her socks, spreading her legs to stretch her calves.

"Nice of you to join us," Christopher said, slinging a bat across his shoulders and twisting at the waist. "Cutting it a little close, aren't you?"

"Don't tell me you were getting nervous?" she asked feigning surprise. "Afraid *you* were going to have to pitch against Brooklyn Tire and Rubber?"

The team laughed because, yeah, the idea of Christopher pitching was that damn funny. He couldn't find the strike zone with GPS. Climbing to her feet, she began stretching her pitching arm.

"We need you on your game today." He took a few practice

swings with the bat. "You know they're going to be riding your ass."

"When am I *not* on my game?" She hated it when Christopher was right. BT&R always gave her shit. *Always.* And if she let those meatheads get in her head today, Mancini's could kiss their record good-bye. "Too bad you can't say the same, coach."

The Mancini's crew had been playing together for a couple of seasons, and the team was accustomed to the endless sarcasm the siblings hurled at one another. It was all in good fun and, as often as not, helped ease the tension before a big game.

Christopher pointed at Jax and told him, "No funny business. I don't know what the beef is with you two, but do not make me sorry I put you on the team."

"Hey, man, I'm just here to play ball," Jax swore, holding up his palms and looking anything but innocent.

When Christopher turned away, he actually had the nerve to wink at her.

And damn if he didn't look good doing it.

"Don't even start," she warned him, realizing too late she was only fueling the fire.

"What?" He climbed to his feet and dusted himself off, his Under Armour shorts doing little to mask that divine butt. "I'm just wondering how the Frankie I knew, a girl who was hands down the clumsiest kid this side of Manhattan, grew up to be Mancini's star pitcher."

"Well, gee, when you put it like that..." She turned and stalked toward the dugout. "You're an ass. You know that, right?" she called over her shoulder, flipping him the bird.

Jax laughed. Of course he did. The guy was like Teflon. Nothing stuck.

"Can't wait to see what you've got, Mancini!"

Blood thrumming through her veins, she didn't bother to look back.

No way in hell would she give him the satisfaction of putting her off-balance, or making her feel like that awkward teen again. She'd grown into her body, and she was the best damn pitcher on the team. Besides, it wasn't like she needed his approval.

Even if it would be sweet revenge to see him eat his words.

A low whistle carried across the field. She cut her eyes at the home team's dugout.

Apparently she had bigger things to worry about than Jackson Hart—like the lunkheads from BT&R who were eyeing her up like a prime side of beef. Meeting their stares, she lifted her chin and slowed her breathing. The last thing she needed was for those jerks to think they'd gotten her hot and bothered.

Once the teams had finished warming up and the coin had been tossed, Becca found herself on the pitcher's mound staring down the third out. Like the three batters before him, he was talking trash and trying to distract her from the runner on second, who seemed to be thinking about stealing third.

Good luck with that. Once the ball crossed home plate, Christopher would be gunning for him.

No, better to focus on her pitches than the runner. He wasn't as fast as he thought he was, and she'd struck out the last two batters with her knuckleball. The current batter had a full count.

Time for a changeup.

"Hey, sweetheart." The batter spit and stepped into the box. "You get me in scoring position, I'll drive you home."

How original.

Thank God she'd skipped lunch or she might've vomited in her mouth.

Gripping the ball tight, she placed her index and middle fingers on the seam as she wound up and let it rip. The ball sailed across the plate, curving to the left as he swung.

Thwump!

The ball hit Christopher's mitt, putting a smile on her face.

"Why you gotta do me like that, baby?" The batter flashed her a smarmy grin, his beady eyes far from amused. Apparently he didn't like striking out with a woman—on or off the field. Fine by her. She didn't like getting hit on by skeezy dirtballs. "You just let me know if you change your mind. I'll see you at the plate."

Becca shuddered and stepped off the pitcher's mound, her cleats digging into the dirt as she made her way across the field. She hated playing BT&R. Most of the guys were cool, but the ones who weren't?

They left her feeling like she'd bathed in a deep fryer.

The team crowded into the dugout, and she found herself on the bench next to Jax.

"Nice pitching." His thigh brushed up against hers, creating a spark of electricity that went straight to her belly. Or maybe it wasn't his touch that had her stomach fluttering but the sheer fact that he'd paid her a compliment. That was probably it. Frankly, it was a wonder he didn't choke on the words. "Can't wait to see what you can do with a bat."

"Looking for pointers?" She smiled sweetly. No way was she going to let Jax get the upper hand again. It was too dangerous—to her resolve and her heart. "I'd be happy to show you a thing or two."

16

JAX

Jax cut his eyes at the pitcher as Becca stepped up to the plate. The guy had been harassing her since she first set foot on the field, and he'd had about enough of it. If that asshole muttered one more sleazy comment—or looked at her ass again—he was going to. Lose. His. Shit.

Trading barbs was part of the game, but there was a fine line between friendly competition and the asshole zone. BT&R's pitcher had crossed it about twenty minutes ago.

Jax hadn't liked him from the outset.

The first time he'd caught that creep staring at Becca's pert little ass in those tiny shorts he'd felt something hot and ugly twisting in his gut.

Climbing to his feet, he hooked his fingers through the chain-link fence that protected the dugout from fly balls.

Becca planted her back foot in the dirt and raised her bat. If it weren't for the tension in her shoulders, she might've looked at ease.

But he knew better. The way she held herself?

It was a sure sign she'd also heard enough from the douchebag on the pitcher's mound.

Actually, he was kind of impressed she hadn't lit the guy up yet. God knew she never missed a chance to tell him where to shove it.

If it went on much longer, he'd step in himself. The guy needed a lesson in manners, and if no one else was up the challenge, he was more than happy to give it.

Chris joined him at the fence. "Give 'em hell, Frankie!"

The ball sailed across the plate, curving to the outside.

Becca held her position.

"Strike!" the ump called.

The team booed, and Jax joined them, knowing full well it was a good call.

Becca adjusted her position.

"What's the deal with this prick?" he asked, nodding at the pitcher. "Things change so much in the last ten years you don't protect your own anymore?"

Chris snorted. "In case you haven't noticed, Frankie's not a kid anymore. She can take care of herself. Watch."

"Tell you what, sweetheart," the pitcher called, his voice carrying across the field. Jax tightened his grip on the fence, the metal digging into his fingers. Who the fuck did this guy think he was? "I'm going to take it easy on you, give it to you straight. You think you can handle it?"

"Less talking, more pitching." Becca narrowed her eyes and dug in her back foot.

The ball sailed over the plate, and true to his word, it was a straight pitch.

She brought her bat around, and it connected with a sharp *crack!* Anyone else would've been swinging for the fences, but not Becca. She nailed a line drive right at the pitcher.

He hit the dirt, landing face first.

Dropping the bat, Becca hauled ass to first, beating the centerfielder's return throw. Dusting her hands off on her shorts, she gave an apologetic shrug to the pitcher that had "sorry, not sorry" written all over it.

Chris smirked. "Like I said."

Jax let out a low whistle. "Remind me not to mess with your sister."

"You kiddin' me?" Chris asked. "She'd rip your nuts off and eat them for breakfast. New York's Bravest? She'd put that shit to the test."

He studied his friend. How would Chris react if he made his intentions known?

Hell, the way he was grinning, maybe he'd already figured it out. "I'm willing to take my chances."

"You and Frankie, huh?" Chris laughed, shaking his head in disbelief. "Good luck, man. That girl goes through men like most women go through friggin' shoes. No guy ever makes it past three dates."

"Three dates?" Good to know. He always worked best with a goal, and the more he could learn about Becca, the better his odds of making it to date number four. Of course, he still needed an official first date, since, orgasms notwithstanding, she wanted nothing to do with him. "I can work with a three-date rule. Anything else I should know?"

17

BECCA

Becca dropped her reusable shopping bags on the floor of the ancient elevator and pushed the button for the fifth floor. The mid-century deathtrap had seen better days, but it beat the hell out of a walkup. It had been weeks since she'd last shopped, and her cabinets were bare. Literally. There wasn't a stale saltine to be found.

She eyed the overflowing bags on the floor. Maybe she'd gone a little overboard, but at least she'd be able to avoid shopping again for a while. Because, although she enjoyed eating, navigating the crowded grocery store made her feel kind of stabby.

It was like her own personal seventh circle of hell.

The doors slid shut, and the car began to rise, chugging noisily toward the fifth floor.

One. Two. Three.

Screech!

The car jerked to a stop, sending her stumbling backward. She grabbed the handrail and pressed herself as flat to the wall as she could manage, holding on for dear life.

Omigod. Omigod. Omigod.

This could not be happening. She was trapped. *Trapped*. In an elevator.

Dangling somewhere between the third and fourth floors.

Alone.

She jabbed the Door Open button. Nothing happened.

She pressed it a dozen more times in rapid succession. Still, nothing happened.

Maybe it was a nightmare.

After all, she'd just blown one hundred dollars on groceries. Nothing said fright night like food shopping and claustrophobia.

She pinched her arm. It hurt like hell, but the scene remained unchanged.

No. Definitely awake.

A fine sweat broke out on her forehead and she pressed her body to the back wall of the elevator, gripping the handrail like her life depended on it.

Because it might.

She sucked in a deep breath, willing herself to remain calm. This wasn't a big deal. She just needed to push the alarm and call for help. That's what you were supposed to do, right?

Peeling her fingers from the handrail, she took two tentative steps across the tiny box and jabbed the alarm button.

A mind-numbing buzz filled the space, droning on endlessly. She glanced at the control panel.

Figured. The old as dirt contraption had no phone and no intercom.

Do. Not. Panic.

Digging through her purse, she searched for her cell phone.

Surely building maintenance could help. Pulling out her phone, she swiped the screen and scrolled through the contacts. Thankfully, she'd actually taken Christopher's advice and programmed the number into her phone when she moved in.

Finding the number, she pushed call and raised the phone to her ear.

Nothing happened.

She glanced at the screen. No signal.

Impossible. In a city of eight million, where every shop, tunnel, and subway car was wired, she was stuck in an elevator with no freaking signal?

Her heart slammed against her rib cage double-time.

Now what?

Was she supposed to just sit there and wait for someone to hear the alarm? It was insanity. She could be stuck for hours.

Sweat trickled down her chest, pooling in the hollow spot between her breasts.

No. There was only one elevator in the building. It wouldn't take long for one of her neighbors to notice that damn buzzing and call for help, right?

Deciding to take matters into her own hands, she stepped up to the door, drew her fist back, and pounded on the door with the heel of her hand. "Help! I'm stuck in the elevator and I can't get out!"

Oh, God. She sounded like one of those awful Life Alert commercials, but what choice did she have?

Swallowing her pride, she pounded away at the door and repeated the cringe worthy plea until she was sure she'd go hoarse.

She checked her watch. Twenty minutes. Twenty minutes of screaming her face off for...*nothing.*

Talk about Murphy's Law.

Any other day she'd have to wait in line for an elevator and pack in with her neighbors like a damn sardine.

Deciding to give her voice a rest, she slumped against the side of the car and pulled a bottle of water from her shopping bag. Time to sit back and let the alarm do its job. Surely someone would come along soon.

Popping the cap, she gulped the water, quenching her thirst and lubricating her sore throat.

Her stomach grumbled, reminding her there was a fresh package of Oreos in the bag. Nothing like a little stress eating to take one's mind off being locked in a dangling deathtrap four floors up.

She opened the package and balanced it on her lap. Grabbing a cookie, she twisted the top off and popped it in her mouth. Then she licked the crème.

She was six cookies deep when she heard a thump on the other side of the door. "Hello? Is someone in there?"

"Yes! Apartment 5C. Please get me out of here," she yelled, clambering to her feet. "I tried to call for help, but I have no signal in here."

"Okay. Don't panic, 5C." *Easy for him to say.* "I'm going to call maintenance."

Five minutes later he returned with bad news. "I left a message with the answering service, but no word yet from maintenance. They suggested I call the fire department."

Son. Of. A. Bitch.

"There must be something else we can do?" she asked, knowing she was being completely illogical. After all, her number one priority was getting the hell out of the elevator.

"Unless you want to hang out for the next few hours waiting for building maintenance to call back, I don't think we have another option," the muffled voice responded. "I'm 4B, by the way. Sorry we have to meet like this."

She wrung her hands.

It was no big deal. There were more firehouses in Brooklyn than she could count.

Besides, for all she knew, Jax wasn't even working.

Keep calm and may the odds be ever in your favor, a sarcastic little voice in her head echoed, reminding her of a popular Facebook meme.

Fat chance.

"Make the call." She slumped to the floor again. "Thanks for helping out, 4B."

Ten minutes later there was another thump on the door. "Miss? This is the New York City Fire Department. We're going to get you out of there, okay?"

"Yes, thank you," she called, stuffing the half-empty Oreo package back in her bag.

No need for anyone else to know about her little cookie binge.

"We've got a team of guys in the lobby and another team heading to the elevator machinery room. Before we get started, can you shut off the alarm for me? Just push the button again. And if you pushed the emergency stop button, I'll need you to disengage that one, too."

She did as he instructed, deactivating the alarm.

The silence was deafening in contrast to the incessant buzzing.

"Great job." Despite the distortion caused by the heavy door, his voice was calm, comforting, and completely unfamiliar. Thank God for small favors. No one would ever have to know about the elevator adventure from hell. "Before my guys do anything else, I need you to try a couple of things for me, okay?"

"Yes." She'd do whatever he asked if it got her out of the sweltering box faster. Her T-shirt clung to her back, and the air had gone from stale to suffocating twenty minutes ago.

"First, why don't you tell me your name so I know who I'm talking to?"

"Becca."

"Becca? This is—"

"Becca?" a second voice cut in. One that was too familiar. One that washed over her like a lover's caress. Stupid Mercury. Stupid retrograde. Erin had warned her to expect the worst, and had she listened? Nope. "Becca, this is Jax. Are you okay?"

"I'm fine," she returned, ignoring the red-hot flush that burned her cheeks. "I'd be better if you could get me the hell out of here."

There was a long pause. Their radios crackled, but it was impossible to make out the words.

The last thing she needed was for Jax to think of her as a damsel in distress. The man already had an ego that exceeded the boundaries of the five boroughs. She *so* didn't need his rescuing.

It wasn't her fault the stupid elevator stalled.

"We'll get you out," the other voice finally responded. "Now I need you to press the Door Open button."

"Yeah, because I haven't tried that yet," she muttered, jabbing the button again with zero expectation of movement. There was a laugh from the other side of the door. Evidently she had a voice that carried. "No dice."

"Okay. We are going to try and recall the elevator to the lobby now with the Firemen Service Override. Hold onto the safety rail, and I'll radio down to the team in the lobby."

The radio crackled again. Thirty seconds passed, and the car didn't so much as budge.

"Becca." It was Jax again. "We've tried all the usual steps to get the elevator moving again, and the service company can't get here for another hour. We are going to cut power to the elevator and pull you out, okay?"

"What? No. No way." She gripped the handrail like a lifeline, an image of the car crashing to the lobby playing on loop in her head. "That sounds like the worst idea ever."

"It's perfectly safe," he promised. Perfectly safe? Nothing

about this felt perfectly safe. Of course, things with Jax rarely did. "The brake will hold the car in place. Removing power is just a safety precaution to ensure there's no movement during extraction."

He seemed to have total confidence in the plan.

Of course he did. He wasn't the one in the fifty-year-old elevator.

"We think you're stuck between three and four, but we need to open the hoistway doors to confirm your exact location," he explained. "You're going to hear the exterior doors opening, so don't panic, okay?"

"Me?" Becca forced a laugh, her belly churning nervously. "Panic?"

18

———

JAX

Once his guys on the roof confirmed they'd locked and tagged the elevator shut-off switch, Jax inserted the drop key in the hoistway door and released the lock. Anderson put pressure on the door, using extreme caution to avoid slipping into the open shaft. The door slid open inch by painstaking inch to reveal the locked inner doors of the car.

Anderson whistled. "Luck be a lady."

Jax grinned. "Piece of cake."

The car hadn't quite reached the fourth floor, stalling about four feet short.

Still, an extraction from above was preferred to one from below as there was no chance of the occupant—of *Becca*—slipping into the shaft. He hated the idea of her stuck in that elevator alone and scared—not that she'd ever admit to being afraid—but they'd have her out in no time.

The key was to remain focused, not let his personal feelings creep in.

The idea of Becca in danger scared the shit out of him. It clawed at his guts, shredding him in a way the flames never could. When he'd pulled up to her building, he'd told himself the odds of finding her in the car were slim. When he'd heard her voice floating through the door, his heart had nearly stopped.

In that moment, he'd realized just how much she meant to him.

Becca was...*everything.*

Everything he'd secretly wanted and never had. Everything he'd never allowed himself to consider. And even though he knew she was perfectly safe in that car, he was anxious, his heart slamming against his rib cage with fury.

He wiped his palms on his navy slacks.

As far as he was concerned, this call couldn't be done fast enough. But rules were rules, and no way was he going to cut corners.

If anything, he'd play it even tighter.

No matter what he was feeling on the inside, the job required complete composure. The people he helped needed to see that he was in control.

Just another day at the office.

"How you doing in there, Becca?" He dropped to a crouch before the door, ensuring she'd be able to see his face when Anderson popped the safety latch.

"Just peachy," came the dry response. "Please, take all the time you need."

A smile tugged at the corner of his mouth. "All right, we're going to open the inner doors now. Go ahead and step toward to the rear wall of the car."

Anderson released the lock and pushed the door open. Then he jammed a chock in the base to ensure they didn't close again.

Becca stood against the rear wall, gripping the safety rail. Under different circumstances, he might've enjoyed that flush in her cheeks, but as it was, it was a far cry from the normal fight response he seemed to draw out of her.

"You know, if you wanted to see me, you could've just called. No need to jam up the elevator like this."

"You're an ass," she said, releasing the railing and drawing herself up to her full height.

And was it a trick of the light, or was that a little spark in her eye?

That's my girl.

"I think you mean I have a nice ass." He winked at her for good measure.

Pissed off Becca trumped frightened Becca any day of the week, even if she was staring him down like he was solely responsible for her current predicament.

"Just my freaking luck." She crossed her arms over her chest and cocked her hip, making it impossible not to notice the way those fitted jeans hugged her curves, accentuating the perfect legs he knew lay beneath the soft fabric. "Ten thousand firemen in New York City and I get the one who'd rather stare at my ass than save it."

"I'd like to think I can do both." He flashed her a cocky grin. "We are New York's Bravest, after all."

"I'll just be over here, pretending I didn't hear any of that," Anderson interjected.

Becca's cheeks turned a deeper shade of crimson. "That's it. I'm leaving town the next time Mercury is in retrograde. This is re-*damn*-diculous." She threw up her hands, seeming to forget her earlier terror. "I hate it when Erin is right."

He didn't know jack about Mercury in retrograde, but that was a conversation for another day. He had a job to do, and the priority was keeping her calm and lucid for what would come next.

"Becca, I need you to focus on me now. I'm going to drop into the elevator with you and then I'm going to lift you out. My partner, Anderson, is going to pull you up."

"You're going to climb in here with me?" she asked, looking doubtful.

He wasn't surprised. In his line of work, he got that question a lot. For many people, it was difficult to comprehend someone willfully entering a dangerous situation others were desperate to escape.

"All in a day's work," he replied with a shrug.

Only today the job was hitting a little close to home.

Lying on his stomach, he slipped his legs through the three-foot opening and lowered himself into the car, extending his arms to their full length. He dropped the last few inches to the floor, doing his best to avoid shaking the car and rattling Becca unnecessarily.

Turning to face her, he offered his hand. "I'm getting you out of here."

"I...can't," she stammered, backpedaling. "What if the elevator drops, like in that movie, and I get chopped in half?" Her eyes darted to the opening between the elevator and the fourth floor. "I really don't want to get chopped in half."

He suppressed a smile. She'd been watching too much TV. Not that he'd done a lot of elevator rescues, but hers wasn't an uncommon fear.

"Look at me, Becca." For once, she did as he asked without arguing. Her eyes locked on his and understanding passed between them. He wouldn't let anything happen to her—not today, not ever. "This elevator isn't going anywhere, which is why we need to get you out."

"Okay." She licked her bottom lip, looking helpless and scared. It was completely at odds with the woman he'd come to know. His gut twisted, and he ached to take her in his arms. "Just...I want you to know I'm sorry. About the radio thing. It was stupid and immature and, well, mean. I'm sorry."

"Apology accepted. Now let's get you out of here." He

grabbed her hand and slipped an arm around her waist, steering her toward the opening. Although he wasn't a fan of his new nickname, he sure as hell didn't have any hard feelings. She'd been angry and hurt and she had every right to feel that way. Besides, this wasn't the time to talk about it. Not when she was scared shitless. "I'm going to boost you up, and Anderson is going to take your hand and pull you out. Got it?"

She drew a shaky breath and nodded. "Fine. But you better keep your hands off my ass if you know what's good for you."

Jax laughed and linked his fingers, creating a step to boost her up to the fourth floor. She placed her left foot in his hands and gripped his shoulders, her nails digging in. When he looked up at her, those dark eyes were swimming with fear.

"You've got this," he promised. She squeezed his shoulder, nodded, and pulled herself up, placing her other foot on the step he'd created. Rising to his full height, he pushed her up and through the opening, keeping his hands off her ass. "You're doing great, Becca. Almost there."

Anderson pulled her over the edge, and she quickly yanked her feet to safety.

Jax grabbed her shopping bags and passed them to Anderson. Then he jumped up and grabbed the edge of the floor, hoisting himself up. He swung a leg up, and using the leverage, heaved himself clear.

Becca sat across the hall with her back to the wall, breathing hard.

"Thank you," she said, clasping her hands between her knees to still their shaking.

"You're welcome. And much as I enjoy the damsel-in-distress routine," he said, settling into the spot beside her, shoulder to shoulder. "I'm going to let you in on a little secret, shortie. A six pack and a hot pie work just as well if you want to woo a firefighter."

19

———

BECCA

BECCA EYED the massive box sticking out of her trunk and sighed. The damn thing was a tighter fit than the L train at rush hour.

So much for doing it on her own. She couldn't even get the stupid thing out of the car by herself.

Now what?

She'd just have to call Christopher. He could help her carry it up, too, since the elevator was still out of service. Not that she was in any great hurry to use it again, but it still chafed a little. Wracking her brain for something she could use to guilt him into helping her, she pulled out her phone and dialed.

"Yo," he answered, a man of few words. How he managed to capture the interest of so many women remained one of the borough's greatest mysteries.

"Hey, Christopher," she said, deciding to play it straight. "Can you get mom to cover the bar for twenty minutes and come help me move a table?"

"It's a little busy right now." He covered the phone and yelled something across the bar before asking her, "Can it wait?"

"Not really. It's sticking out the back of my car, and I don't want it to walk off while I'm upstairs." She left off the part where she'd been too cheap to pay fifty-nine dollars for delivery. After all, that's why God gave her a strapping older brother, right? She sighed heavily, making sure her next words were laden with the remnants of teenage angst. "Remember that time you told Jimmy Sanders I had lice, and he refused to sit next to me in class for a week?" She sniffed for effect.

Really, she should get an Oscar nod for these performances.

"All right, all right. Let me go talk to Ma. I'll be there in ten."

Becca disconnected and slipped the phone in her pocket.

God help her the day she ran out of ways to manipulate Christopher.

Fortunately, he'd given her lots of ammunition during their formative years. Little did he know she hated sitting next to Jimmy Sanders. The kid smelled like boiled cabbage, and the week he'd refused to sit next to her had been like heaven.

Climbing up on the hood of her car, she sat to wait for the muscle.

It was a beautiful evening, way too nice to wait inside. Plus, it was unlikely Christopher would be on time. Ten minutes probably meant fifteen, because if she knew her brother at all, being busy meant he was scoring digits.

Ten minutes later a black SUV pulled up to the curb. She ignored it at first, but when Jax stepped out, looking sexy as hell and smug to boot, her temper flared.

Christopher had sold her out.

"What are you doing here?" she asked, sliding off the car and going on the offensive.

"Chris said you needed a hand. He was busy, so I volunteered." He shrugged like it was no big deal.

But it was. It was a big freaking deal. Especially after the elevator debacle.

While she'd been on the verge of losing it, he'd been so calm and controlled.

Putting her at ease and risking his own safety to protect her? That was a side of Jax she wouldn't—*couldn't*— consider. Because if she thought for one second that he'd actually changed, she might go and do something stupid like fall in love with him again.

He circled her tiny Honda, stopping at the open trunk.

"You were at Mancini's?"

"I like to support local businesses," he responded, gripping the end of the box and shifting the weight to free it from the tiny vehicle.

Figured. Just like its owner, it moved instantly at his touch.

Whoa. Strike that. Jackson Hart did not *move* her. And if he did, the only place she was going was Aggravation Station, population one.

"Really?" she asked, her words dripping with sarcasm. "You just happened to be hanging out at Mancini's?"

"What can I say?" He slid the box out of the trunk and stood it on its end, leaning on the top and showcasing those ridiculous biceps of his. Her traitorous heart fluttered at the sight. "Your mom makes the best sauce in Brooklyn."

Jax was making himself right at home in her life again.

It was too familiar. Too dangerous.

"Convenient excuse." She slammed the trunk, her purse sliding off the roof of the car and landing on the blacktop.

"Excuse?" he asked, shifting his face into a mask of confusion. As if he didn't know exactly what she meant.

"For completely invading my life." She raised her brows and looked around. What was this, the third time he'd been to her apartment uninvited? "You're worse than a bad penny, showing up every time I turn around."

"So you *don't* want me to take the table upstairs?" he asked with a lazy grin, not the least bit offended by her insinuation.

"No. Yes." She pinched the bridge of her nose. Why did she let herself get so flustered around him? Deep cleansing breaths —that's what she needed. She bent over and picked up her purse, knowing full well he was staring at her butt. Stupid yoga pants. Returning to an upright position, she slung her bag over her shoulder. "I mean, quit following me."

"Just to be clear." He leaned forward so close their lips were almost touching. She could smell peppermint on his breath, one of the starlight mints from Mancini's. "I'm more than happy to lead if you want to try following."

"You're impossible." Turning on her heel, she stomped up the stairs and opened the front door. "You first. I'm not walking up five flights of stairs with you ogling my ass."

He breezed by as if the table weighed nothing at all. "Fine by me. I don't mind if you stare at my ass. Actually, I think I'll rather enjoy it, knowing you're getting as hot for me as I am for you."

She climbed the stairs, telling herself it was the exercise, not the man above, heating her skin.

So what if he had a perfect ass, the kind that was round and firm and looked like you could bounce quarters off it. There was nothing wrong with liking his ass, right? Butt lust was harmless.

She liked Channing Tatum's ass, and she was in no danger of falling into bed with him.

Jax stopped at the fifth-floor landing, waiting for her outside her apartment door.

And of course, he wasn't even out of breath, while she was huffing and puffing like she'd just run the New York City Marathon.

Cursing herself for noticing the way his pecs contracted when he picked up the box, she unlocked the door and pushed it wide, allowing him to enter first.

"Where do you want me to put it?"

She groaned. That was the sixty-four-thousand-dollar question, wasn't it?

20

———

JAX

Jax set the monstrous box on the floor in the dining space and pulled out his Swiss Army knife, making quick work of the packing tape. One look at the directions and he knew he was in trouble. Apparently the Swedes didn't believe in step-by-step instructions, just poorly drawn depictions of furniture that seemed only loosely based on the actual design.

Who the hell bought flat pack furniture anyway?

The answer was five foot eight and staring him down with a pair of bourbon-colored eyes that could blitz his control faster than the contents of any bottle. Wearing a pair of black knee-length stretch pants that hugged every curve, and an off the shoulder Supergirl T-shirt that revealed the supple skin of her neck, she was definitely putting his control to the test. He wanted nothing more than to lick that stretch of bare skin while she moaned with pleasure.

"Well, aren't you just a regular MacGyver." She kicked off her black and white Chuck Taylors and leaned against the back of the overstuffed purple loveseat that separated the tiny living and dining spaces.

"I always wanted to be a boy scout." He rolled his shoulders and fished the bag of hardware out of the box. Time to focus on the task at hand. "Never stayed in one place long enough to join, but I like to think I've got the whole 'be prepared' thing down."

"Prepared, indeed." An amused smile lit up her face. She crossed her legs, drawing his gaze up the long line of her body. Fucking perfect. From her bare feet to the curve of her hips to the swell of her breasts. There wasn't a thing he would change, except, maybe, her opinion of him. That alone should have been reason enough to steer clear of her. His job was too dangerous for him to consider a serious relationship. Growing up he'd seen firsthand what kind of fallout it could bring. "You do know I'm capable of putting my own table together, right?"

He snorted, ignoring the thinly veiled suggestion to leave. "Shortie, you do know grown adults shouldn't buy imported, DIY furniture, right?" If it weren't for him, she'd still be downstairs wrestling the monstrosity out of that munchkin-mobile she called a car. "The Brooklyn Flea has real furniture with twice as much charm as this big box stuff."

"Cute," she drawled, twisting her wild curls up and pinning them atop her head. "Don't tell me you're intimidated by a little DIY? Or are you having trouble with the directions? Not enough pictures for you?"

He balled up the assembly instructions—they weren't going to be much help anyway—and threw them back in the box, loving the way her eyebrows shot up in alarm.

"What do you think you're doing?" Falling to her knees, she grabbed the wadded-up mess and tried unsuccessfully to flatten it out. "We need to follow the directions."

"You? Follow directions?" Unlikely. From what he'd seen, she was more likely to issue them than take them. "It's fine. I've got this."

"All right, macho man. Have it your way." She crossed her

legs and settled back to watch, apparently deciding to let him have a go at it. "But if it falls apart, I'm holding you responsible."

"It's a table. How hard can it be?"

She smirked, her words taking on a playful edge. "Do you really want me to answer that?"

No, he really didn't. If she went down that path, he'd feel inclined to show her right there on the dining room floor how hard it could be, and the damn table might never get assembled.

Forty minutes and a whole lot of aggravation later, he tightened the last screw, claiming victory.

"It's perfect," Becca said, running her hand lovingly over the smooth surface.

"I'm still trying to figure out why it has six legs." He scratched the back of his head, studying the crisscrossing supports.

"It's stylish."

Hardly. The table legs were exactly where the human ones should go during a meal.

A guy like him? He'd be kicking them all through dinner. "It lacks function."

"Tomato, tomahto." She hopped up on the table, her thighs spreading modestly as her legs dangled over the side. Blood rushed to his cock. Did she have any idea of the effect she had on him? "Seems pretty functional to me."

"Looks can be deceiving." He took a step toward the table. The conversation was shifting, like it always did, no matter how hard she tried to fight this thing between them. Gone were the combative undertones. They'd been replaced with a tension so thick he was choking on it, desperate to crush his lips to hers and inhale the intoxicating scent that made his body throb with need. "There's only one way to know for sure."

"Oh?" It wasn't so much a question as a breathy whisper rolling off her full lips.

"Put it to the test." He took a step closer. Her knees brushed his thighs, but she held her ground, keeping him at a distance.

"Wh-what are you suggesting?"

"I'm suggesting"—he ran his palms up her soft thighs, spreading them wide—"I'd like to lay you out right here on the table and work that sweet little body of yours until you're writhing in ecstasy, back bowed and screaming my name."

Spreading her legs wider, she granted him better access, her breasts rising and falling rapidly. "Think your craftsmanship can handle it?"

"I'm pretty confident in my craftsmanship." She wanted a challenge? He'd give her one. He positioned himself between her legs and cupped her chin, tilting it to him. "The real question is, can *you* handle it?"

Gripping the front of his T-shirt, she twisted her fingers in the soft material and pulled him closer, bridging the gap between them and bringing her lips to his ear. "What's it going to take to show you I'm a big girl, Jax?"

Her tongue darted out, teasing his earlobe and making his balls draw up so damn tight they ached.

Then she bit him. Fucking *bit* him.

And he loved it, an erotic wave of pleasure/pain rushing straight to his gut and unleashing a riptide of desire.

He reached for her hips and pulled her to the edge of the table, letting her feel the hard ridge of his erection against her belly. Lowering his mouth to hers, he licked her bottom lip, sucking it into his mouth.

She moaned quietly, shifting her hips and locking her ankles around his back.

Like before, she responded explosively, melding her mouth to his and mating her tongue with his own.

"More," she panted, breaking away and pulling his shirt over his head. Then she stripped away her own tee, revealing the perky breasts he'd been dreaming of for the last damn week. "I need more."

Shit. The way she was looking at him, like she wanted to devour him whole, he'd give her whatever she wanted. No questions asked.

She skimmed her fingers over his abs, her hands leaving a blaze in their wake as they moved north, skating over his pecs. And like a greedy bastard, he stood there basking in her glow, enjoying the fire of her touch as she explored his body.

Stretching up, she kissed him, working his lips feverishly as she unbuckled his belt and drew his zipper down, freeing his erection.

He tensed at her touch.

"Don't worry." She stroked his length, her fingers sliding up and down like silk despite her firm grip. "I'll be gentle," she promised, rubbing her thumb in a circular motion over the slick head.

He groaned. If she kept this up, he wasn't going to last long.

Then, as if determined to test his restraint, she brought her thumb to her lips and licked it.

When she looked up at him from beneath her lashes, with something dark and hungry reflected in her eyes, he abandoned any semblance of control. Lifting her bottom from the table, he removed the rest of her clothes, leaving her naked, flawless and splayed out before him like a feast.

A very sweet, very innocent feast. Right up until she reached down and started stroking her clit.

Then she looked downright sexy, driving him mad with lust.

"I need to be inside you," he said, stroking his cock and pumping into his own hand. "I need it fast and hard and sweaty."

Her eyes lit up at the proposition and a wicked grin spread over her face. "I wouldn't have it any other way."

Grabbing a condom from his wallet, he rolled it on, thankful he was prepared in more ways than one.

Becca wrapped her legs around him, giving him complete control of her body as he drove into her, burying himself to the hilt. She gripped his shoulders, her nails digging into his back as he withdrew and thrust into her over and over, pushing them both toward oblivion.

He hadn't expected this favor to end with an orgasm, but he wasn't complaining.

Being with Becca? It was like nothing he'd ever experienced. The way she responded to his touch spoke a hell of a lot louder than the endless snark she dished out. And one way or another, he'd prove to her that he'd changed.

He wasn't the same kid who'd left town without saying goodbye, and whether she realized it or not, she could count on him for a hell of a lot more than a good time.

"Jax," she panted, burying her face in his shoulder. "I'm going to come."

He cupped her ass, holding her body flush as their hips crashed together, tension coiling low in his gut.

A few more strokes and she was chanting his name like a prayer.

Her teeth clamped down on his shoulder, sending him over the edge, his own orgasm searing through his body like a four-alarm fire. A shudder ran down his spine, but he held her tight, savoring the moment, knowing it would end too soon.

Any minute now reality would come crashing back, and she'd remember all the reasons she couldn't— wouldn't —trust him.

"Looks like you were wrong about the table after all," she whispered.

"I have to admit it's pretty sturdy for an import." Finding her mouth with his own, he kissed her slow and deep. "But if this is what it feels like to be wrong, well, give me a few minutes and I could be wrong all over again. What do you say?"

"What do I say?" She looked up at him with wide eyes and scooted off the table, forcing him to take a step back. "I say it's time to pack up your hose and go. I, um, have work to do."

Not again.

He watched in disbelief as she gathered her clothes and headed for the bedroom, shutting the door very deliberately behind her.

So much for beating her at her own game.

21

BECCA

BECCA TOOK an empty seat at the end of the wooden sushi bar and checked her watch. If Erin was crossing the Brooklyn Bridge —*and* buying lunch at Sushi Katsuei—she was up to something. And whatever it was, it felt big.

She drummed her fingers on the counter while she waited, thoughts of Jax creeping in as they always did when her brain was idle. Which was exactly why she'd been keeping busy, busy, busy. The last thing she needed to do was spend any more time thinking about *him.*

Even if he had given her the best orgasms of her life.

Still, he was infuriating and pushy, and she didn't need him invading her life or her brain or her panties. No, what she needed was to focus on her photography. Her time would be much better spent trying to figure out how to leverage the FDNY Calendar of Heroes into something bigger, because what she really needed was more freelance work to build her portfolio.

And more of those mind-blowing orgasms.

Where the hell had that come from?

She cringed and shook her head, attempting to clear her thoughts.

After giving Jax the post-coital brush off—*again*—the odds were pretty good he was done handing out orgasms. To her, anyway. The other four million women in New York City? They were probably fair game. And that's what she wanted, wasn't it?

So why did the idea of Jax moving on to someone else leave such a sour taste in her mouth?

Thankfully, Erin breezed into the tiny restaurant, providing a much-needed distraction.

"Sorry I'm late," Erin said, taking the empty stool to Becca's right. "I always forget how long it takes to get to Brooklyn."

Becca grinned. Manhattanites acted like Brooklyn was an entirely different country, when in reality it was a twenty-minute ride on the subway, a trip she made twice a day Monday through Friday.

Once they'd ordered a variety of sushi rolls, Erin was ready to talk business.

"So, did you see the article I wrote on the models from the FDNY Calendar of Heroes?"

Had she seen it? The article had set off a firestorm among Erin's female readership. "Of course I saw it. I think every woman in Manhattan commented on that article," she teased.

"Exactly," Erin said, flipping her hair over her shoulder. "I swear when I write about serious matters, no one gives a damn, but throw in hot, sexy dudes and my reach grows exponentially."

"I'm not so sure that's actually a good thing."

"Tell me about it." Erin snorted. "But I'm a woman of the people, and I intend to give them more of what they want. They've made it quite clear they want a series featuring those sexy firefighters."

"How does your editor feel about this?"

It was hard to imagine the magazine approving an entire series dedicated to a shirtless FDNY. Besides, Erin tended to favor serious, investigative pieces, and this pitch sounded a lot like fluff.

Erin waved dismissively. "I'll get her on board. Besides, I fully intend the whole thing to culminate in a piece of legitimate journalism about the danger of their work. They may be hot, but those guys really are heroes."

"So part human interest, part profile, part news story?"

"Exactly." Erin grinned from ear to ear, scooting her stool closer. "Each week I'll profile a couple of guys, which I can do one-on-one, but I'll also need access to a firehouse to really get the 'day in the life' angle right."

"Sounds like you've got it all figured out," she said, wondering once again why Erin had asked her to lunch. Clearly she was missing something, a key element to the plan.

"Almost." Erin paused as their plates were delivered. "*Arigatou*," she said, thanking the sushi chef, before returning her attention to Becca.

"Why do I get the feeling I'm not going to like where this is going?"

"Probably because you're a spoilsport." Erin popped a sushi roll into her mouth, chewing slowly. "Huh. This is pretty damn good." She studied her plate. "Great balance of texture and flavor. Who knew you could get sushi like this in Brooklyn?"

Becca rolled her eyes and selected a spicy tuna roll from the plate, dipping it in soy sauce before raising it to her mouth.

Erin used the back end of her chopsticks to remove another roll from their shared plate. "I want you to convince Jax to let you do a ride along with his company."

"No way." She dropped her chopsticks and abandoned any pretense of etiquette. "Uh, uh. I told you. He's trouble."

Erin arched her brow.

"I kind of had sex with him again." She closed her eyes, guilt crushing her like an anvil. "And then kicked him out."

"Again? Please tell me he wasn't naked this time?" she asked, a pinched look contorting her face. "Seriously. What is wrong with you?"

She sighed. Erin wouldn't understand. The other woman had never had her heart ripped out by the opposite sex.

Finally, she just went with the old standby. "It's complicated."

"It always is." Erin rubbed her forehead, shedding her best friend role and slipping into that of Back-alley O'Malley, all tough love and hard facts. "Never mind. Whatever weird sex thing you two have going on is personal. This is business. You want to get your photography business off the ground? This is your chance."

"Whatever," she said, crossing her arms. No way in hell was she asking Jax for a ride along. Or anything else, for that matter. No. Way. Erin remained silent, staring at her expectantly. "You're the writer. Shouldn't you go? You know, to get all the facts and whatnot?"

"Come on, Becca. A picture is worth a thousand words. I can make magic with a twenty-minute interview, but what you can do with a camera? Those images will bring their stories to life." Erin paused before pulling her trump card. "Besides, it pays."

Well, shit. That changed everything, didn't it?

"Since when do you turn down freelance work?" Erin asked, grinning triumphantly.

"I don't." Her shoulders slumped. Sometimes being a grown-up sucked monkey balls. She needed the money and the photo credits. There was no way she could turn the job down, even if it meant asking Jax for a favor. "What exactly do I have to do?"

22

—————

JAX

Jax was finishing up the daily equipment check, ensuring all the guys had their gear clean and operational, when O'Rourke entered the apparatus bay.

"Hey, Lieutenant. You, uh, got a visitor." O'Rourke stuffed his hands in his pockets.

Whoever it was, they made the kid nervous. FDNY brass? Seemed unlikely. Especially unannounced at seven thirty in the morning.

"A visitor?" he asked, signing off on the log and signaling the guys to begin loading their equipment for the day's shift. "Who is it?"

"Don't shoot the messenger," the kid responded, sliding his gaze toward the bay doors. "She was pretty insistent. Wouldn't take no for an answer."

"She?" He stepped out from behind the apparatus to see Becca standing there with two white bakery boxes, smiling sweet as you please. Which made zero sense, since she'd made it perfectly clear—every chance she got—they had no future.

So what the hell was she doing at the firehouse?

"Thanks." He handed O'Rourke the clipboard. "I'll take care of this."

"The Hartbreak Kid rides again!" Anderson called, abandoning any pretense of loading gear. "Think you'll get another radio spot?"

Jax flipped him off.

Becca kept that charming smile fixed on her face as he approached, but her eyes were wary. Perhaps she was wondering if he was going to let her have it in front of the entire company. There was no way she hadn't heard Anderson's jokes.

Or his delightful new nickname.

After everything she'd put him through, he'd be well within his right to ask her to leave. But no, he wasn't angry. Just curious. He had yet to figure out exactly what was going on in that pretty little head of hers.

Maybe if he played his cards right, she'd clue him in.

"Good morning." She shifted her weight and peeked over his shoulder at the crew of firemen who were no doubt watching their exchange with rabid interest.

"What brings you to the neighborhood?" he asked, wishing O'Rourke hadn't brought her to the bay. He didn't want an audience, but more importantly, he didn't want the guys staring at those fucking perfect legs. The skirt she wore ended just above the knee, but as far as he was concerned it was NSFW. "We don't usually get visitors so early."

"I was on my way to work, and I wanted to drop off some homemade desserts for the guys," she explained, thrusting the white boxes into his chest and leaving him with no choice but to accept them. She offered a tentative smile, looking up at him from under her lashes. "To say thank you for...helping me. With the whole elevator thing. Italian cookies and tiramisu."

There was more to this visit than a simple thank-you. She was nervous. And rambling. What was she up to now?

He remained silent, determined to let her sweat it out.

"I'm sure they'll be a hit," she said, rubbing her palms together. Her gaze traveled around the apparatus bay before returning to him. "Mom made them."

"Thank you. These guys love a good dessert." He turned, as if to end the conversation. "See you around."

"Wait." She reached out, grabbing his forearm. "There's something else."

He'd suspected as much.

She chewed her bottom lip, looking unsure of herself. "I need a favor."

"A favor?" he asked, feigning disbelief and enjoying the flash of annoyance in her eyes. "From me?"

"Don't let it go to your head." She crossed her arms and lifted her chin. "Erin's doing another piece on the FDNY. Part human interest, part news. The magazine hired me to shoot the series, but I need permission to ride along."

"And since I'm the only fireman you know, you were hoping I could help you out?"

She sighed, letting him know exactly how she felt about the prospect, and nodded.

Laughter bubbled up from his gut. Irony was a bitch. "Let me get this straight. Now you want to invade my life and follow *me* around?"

"It's strictly professional," she bit out through clenched teeth.

It was probably killing her to ask this favor of him, given her proud nature. Just another thing they had in common. He hated asking for help himself.

Of course, that didn't mean he couldn't have a little fun with her.

"I don't know. A ride along?" He rubbed the back of his neck, pretending to think it over. "That's a pretty big ask."

"Come on, Jax. Don't be a jerk." She tucked a curl behind her ear and licked her lips again. "I need this job."

"I know," he said, unable to resist goading her a little bit. "That's why I'm going to need you to ask me nicely. Maybe even throw in some flattery."

"Listen, stud. That dessert?" She raised her brow and nodded at the white boxes. "That's tantamount to begging. But if you're not interested..." She glanced over his shoulder and unbuttoned the top button of her blouse, putting his dick on high alert. "I'll find someone who is."

Over his dead body.

"In fact, I think O'Rourke kind of likes me." She waved, and dammit if O'Rourke wasn't returning the gesture, cheeks burning bright.

"Don't get too excited." He widened his stance and planted his hands on his hips, blocking her view and cutting off the amateur hour flirt fest. "O'Rourke likes all women. The kid doesn't exactly discriminate."

"Perfect." Beaming up at him, she called his bluff. "Then he won't be hard to convince."

With a determined look in her eye, she sashayed across the bay, wiggling her ass with each step.

Well, shit. That had backfired, hadn't it?

"Oh, no you don't, shortie." He chased her down, cutting off her path. The only firefighter she was going to be riding with was him. "I'll need to get it cleared with the captain." He winked at her, knowing it would just rile her up more. "By the way, I like it when you fight dirty."

23

BECCA

BECCA PULLED up to the curb at St. John's Place with her stomach in her throat. There was a very real possibility she was going to spew granola cereal all over the car if she didn't get her nerves settled. The prospect of spending forty-eight hours at the station with Jax?

Yeah, that had her belly twisted in knots.

Really. Big. Knots.

What the hell had she gotten herself into?

Throwing the car into park, she leaned back against the headrest. When she'd received the text from Jax saying her ride along had been approved, she'd had mixed emotions. Half of her wanted to celebrate, the other half wanted to scream.

Today the screaming side was winning out.

Get it together. You want to be treated like a professional? Act like one.

She opened one eye and peeked at the firehouse. Unlike her last visit, the bay doors were down. There were two of them, one labeled Ladder One-Three-Two and one labeled Engine Two-Eight-Oh. Both were painted with the words "In the Eye of the Storm."

Nice. Nothing said, "Welcome to Brooklyn," like a burning skull and crossbones.

Suck it up. It's time to get this show on the road.

Thirty minutes later she found herself on a whirlwind tour of the firehouse with Jax.

Thankfully, she didn't have to ask a lot of questions. He was incredibly knowledgeable and more than willing to share, giving her a full history of the company, a rundown on the equipment, and a real understanding of a day in the life of New York's Bravest. Mostly she just listened and snapped pictures, absorbing as much information as possible to feed back to Erin for the series.

It was fascinating.

There was so much she didn't know, like the difference between a ladder company and an engine company, and the fact that they were housed together to work in tandem.

Much as she hated to admit it, she was actually impressed to learn Jax worked on a ladder truck.

He and his crew were the first through the door doing forcible entry and search and rescue.

Talk about courage.

Heck, she'd nearly had a nervous breakdown just being trapped in an elevator. She couldn't even begin to guess at the mettle it took to charge into a fire, risking his life to save another. It was the very definition of selfless, something she had a hard time associating with the kid who'd left her high and dry.

Maybe he really had changed.

Or maybe he was just one of those adrenaline junkies with a hero complex.

She watched silently as he demonstrated the proper way to put on turnout gear over his fitted cotton uniform. So patient. So self-assured. *So damn gorgeous.*

Yeah, she could totally see why women threw their panties at men in uniform.

Hell, the man in question pushed her bitch buttons like no other, but that didn't stop him from setting her panties on fire.

"Hey," Jax asked, resting a hand on her shoulder. "You still with me?"

"Huh?" She blinked. "Sorry. What were you saying?"

He stripped off the black jacket and placed it back on the rack. "I was just saying that fully dressed with gear, each man on the truck is toting an extra seventy-five pounds in personal protective equipment."

"Guess that explains all the muscles," she quipped, giving herself a mental face palm as soon as the words were out. Where was her filter this morning? The last thing she needed was for him to think she was distracted by his stupid muscles. "Not that I was looking."

He flashed those damn dimples. "*Riiiight.*"

"So what made you decide to become a firefighter, anyway?" she asked, changing the subject to something less volatile than his orgasm-inducing body. "Please tell me you didn't do it just to meet women."

He smiled at her joke, but it didn't reach his eyes. No, his eyes were sad, as if she'd touched on an old wound. "I guess you didn't know this. I don't talk about it much, but I lost my mom to a house fire."

Shit.

He scrubbed a hand over his face. "My old man was working out of town, and we were staying with my aunt. She left a candle burning overnight, and the whole place went up in flames. The firemen were able to get my aunt and me out, but it was too late for my mom. I was three at the time."

"I'm so sorry, Jax."

"It was a long time ago." He shoved his hands into his pockets. "I'm ashamed to admit it, but I can hardly remember her. I've got some old pictures..."

"But it's not the same."

"No, it's not the same." He forced a smile. "Anyway, I've always known I wanted to be a firefighter, to save lives, and that's what keeps me going. If I can spare even one child that kind of loss? It's all worth it. That's why I got the tattoo," he said, pointing to his right shoulder. Although it was covered by his uniform, she could see the flames in her mind's eye, wrapping around his bicep and shoulder as if to consume him. "So I'll never forget."

Her heart broke for the boy who'd lost his mother so tragically. And for the man who needed so desperately to save others from the thing that scared him most.

What a heavy burden to carry day in and day out.

She'd always known his home life was tough, but he'd been tightlipped about it as a kid. He hadn't wanted their pity then, and he wouldn't want it now.

"I'm sure she's very proud of you." She reached out and straightened his collar, running her fingers over the silver axe insignia. This was one story that would stay off the record. There were some things more sacred than a byline. "Tell me, how many lives have you saved, Jax?"

"You don't keep track of the ones who live, the ones who go home to their families and thank God above." He met her gaze, his eyes as hard as ice, his words wrought with conviction. "You remember the ones you've lost, the ones you couldn't save. And you pray like hell the next time you'll be faster, stronger, and luckier."

Spoken like a true hero.

Her gut clenched. She'd been so incredibly wrong about Jackson Hart. And that was dangerous. So very dangerous.

Protecting her heart from an arrogant prick would be a walk in the park, but a man like this? One who embraced life to the fullest? One who put his life on the line everyday so that others could live?

That would be a hell of a lot harder.

24

JAX

Jax filled two mugs with coffee and offered one to Becca, joining her at the kitchen table. Their time in the apparatus bay had left him raw and exposed. What he needed now was a few minutes to collect his thoughts and get his head on straight.

Giving Becca a tour of the station had seemed harmless enough, but he'd quickly discovered that the more he talked, the more questions she had.

He'd forgotten how inquisitive she could be. Every question she asked opened the door to another, and some doors he preferred to keep closed.

And seeing her with her camera—she was focused, driven, determined.

It was a total turn-on, and he had no doubt the piece would be amazing.

The real concern was having her under his roof for two days. There was no escape for either of them, and while he'd spent the last few weeks trying to reconnect with her, he'd never considered the possibility that she might slip past his barriers in the process. He hadn't meant to tell her about his mom—the last thing he wanted was her pity—but it had just tumbled out of his mouth. Having her immersed in his world without her usual snark and sass?

It was fucking *uncomfortable*.

He drank his coffee black, noting Becca added both cream and sugar to hers before taking the first sip.

"Real mugs? How environmentally friendly." She set her coffee on the table, keeping her fingers wrapped around the handle.

He grinned. "It's tradition. Besides, most of us spend four days a week at the firehouse. That means it needs to be comfortable. This place is a second home for most of us."

"I hadn't thought about it like that," she said, surveying the kitchen as if seeing it for the first time. "Then I guess that makes you all family."

"Pretty much," he agreed. "Being a firefighter? It's not just a job. It's *the* job. It's a lifestyle."

"Ah, yes," she said, bobbing her head and tapping her chin. "Now I remember. The badge comes with a healthy dose of ego, too."

"If the boot fits." He raised his mug in salute, hoping to steer the conversation back to her. He didn't want to talk about the demands of the job. She might not understand. It wasn't just hard on the firefighter, it was hard on the people they loved, too. "What about you?"

"Me?" She laughed. "My ego pales in comparison to yours."

"Cute." He reached across the table and covered her hand with his own. "I meant, tell me more about your photography. You said you were interested in photojournalism, right?"

"I'm surprised you remembered."

"I remember everything when it comes to you, but I have to be honest, I have no idea how photojournalism is different than traditional photography."

She leaned forward, her face lighting up. "It's just a fancy way of saying that I want to photograph real life, unfiltered. Instead of people posturing and posing, I want to catch the action as it unfolds, capturing those candid shots that reflect true emotion."

"So following a bunch of truckies around is right up your alley then."

"Yes and no." She frowned, studying him thoughtfully. "I wouldn't shy away from a fire if the situation presented itself, but I wouldn't wish for tragedy just to round out my portfolio. I'd be just as happy sitting around the station for two days, knowing you're not barreling into a burning building with nothing more than an air tank, an axe, and the world's biggest ego."

"So you do care," he teased, wiggling his eyebrows. "I knew you'd come around eventually."

"Are you always in the habit of flattering yourself? Because that explains a lot," she said, collecting his mug with a grin and turning to the sink. "I just meant that I'm working on a special piece right now." Turning on the water, she went to work washing up. "It's sort of an effervescent and macabre look at life in New York. I need a few more images, but it's almost finished."

He moved to the sink, leaning against the counter next to her. "I'd love to see it when it's ready."

"I don't think so," she said, keeping her attention focused on the soapy dish. "I'm not really comfortable sharing my work."

"Let me get this straight," he said, handing her a towel to dry her hands. When she turned from the sink, he was there, blocking her retreat. "You trust me with your body, but not your art?"

"It's personal."

"Personal?" He braced his hands on the counter, backing her up against the sink. Her breathing came fast and furious as she looked up at him with those big brown eyes. "I've buried myself so deep between your thighs I couldn't tell where my body ended and yours began. It doesn't get more personal than that."

Shifting her weight, she hooked her fingers in the waistband of his pants, her thighs brushing his as she stretched up on her toes and lifted her chin.

Just as she was about to press those sweet lips to his, the alarm ripped through the station.

25

BECCA

Becca froze, stopping short of kissing Jax. The screeching alarm cut through...whatever the hell it was she was doing, yanking her back to reality. The place where she and Jax were not supposed to be kissing anymore.

"Duty calls." He grabbed her hand and pulled her toward the stairs, descending at a breakneck pace.

Adrenaline coursed through her, propelling her forward.

Whether it was Jax's touch or the bleating alarm that sent her body into overdrive, she couldn't be sure. His hand was strong and sure as he led her to the apparatus bay, positioning her out of the way as he jumped into his turnout gear.

It was chaos. Organized chaos, but chaos nonetheless with men swarming the bay.

For a second, she just watched as the firefighters donned their gear, boots first.

Then instinct kicked in. She had a job to do.

Focusing her camera, she began snapping photos, stopping only when they were all dressed and climbing into the truck.

Jax hoisted her up, taking the seat opposite. Their knees brushed, but he didn't even look her way, just banged his hand on the outside of the rig, signaling the driver—no, the "chauffer"—they were ready to roll.

The truck's siren blared, nearly shattering her eardrums as they pulled out onto the street, followed by engine two-eighty.

Jax slipped his helmet on and, noticing Becca staring, squeezed her knee.

Did he think she was scared? She wasn't. More like shocked.

He was a freaking officer. A lieutenant. He'd completely downplayed his role when he'd told her family—told her—he was a firefighter. And that humility?

It was completely at odds with the bravado he wore most days.

The truck sailed through traffic, sirens screaming.

She glanced out the window at the Prospect Heights neighborhood sliding past in a blur. No wonder they called the driver a chauffeur. The man could seriously drive, handling the truck like a damn Maserati, hauling ass across town.

"All right, captain, what're we looking at?" Jax shouted.

"Mid-rise apartment fire. Probably going to be a two-alarm, but we'll call it at the scene."

"Fully involved?" he asked, his mouth a grim line.

"Not yet. We're going straight in."

Jax and his men started strategizing, discussing how they'd attack the fire and which role each would take. She didn't understand most of it, but what she did catch made her heart leap into her throat.

Lifting her camera, she captured the face of each man that would be rushing into the blaze.

Anderson would be on the roof, checking it for stability. O'Rourke would be venting the upper levels, ensuring the smoke had an egress point. And Jax? He was the irons man, leading a rescue team to search for survivors who might be trapped inside.

It scared the crap out of her.

This is what they do. Every day. When duty calls.

The men were out the door before the truck rolled to a stop. They had jobs to do, and so did she.

Sucking in a deep breath, she followed them, snapping shots of the building and the commotion on the ground as soon as her sneakers hit the pavement.

"Stay behind the fire line." Jax grabbed her shoulders, forcing her to look him in the eye. Despite the gravity of the situation, he was in complete control, just as he'd been when he pulled her out of the elevator. "Do not leave the tuck. Understand?"

Did he think she had a death wish?

She nodded, and he took off, huddling quickly with his men before deciding on a point of entry.

The lower level of the stone building was fully engulfed in flames. Smoke poured from the upper windows. The engine company was laying out their hoses and charging the lines, preparing to attack the fire on the main floor.

An ambulance arrived on the scene, siren wailing and lights flashing.

"Surround and drown!" the engine captain hollered.

Focusing on her own job, she began snapping photos. Her hands were shaking so damn bad she nearly dropped the camera, but she pressed on.

Anderson climbed into the bucket and ascended skyward. *Click.*

He climbed onto the roof and disappeared from view. *Click.*

An older gentleman waved from a third-floor window, begging for help. A ladder went up, and a firefighter scaled the rungs to assist in the evacuation. *Click.*

There were several residents standing on the curb across the street, watching in shock as their homes burned. *Click.*

She tried to block out their grief and do her job. They had a story to tell and her photos would give them a voice.

Click. Click. Click.

She lost track of time, completely immersed in the scene around her. The tension on the street was palpable as the Bravest fought to bring the blaze under control.

Another engine pulled up to the scene and her chest tightened.

Where the hell was Jax? Using her lens, she zeroed in on the men racing up and down the ladders.

No Jax.

Was he inside? Was he okay? What if he'd been trapped by the flames?

She couldn't be sure, but it seemed they'd grown, despite the steady stream of water the engine was pumping into the building.

Radios crackled, barely audible over the spray of the hoses and the shouts of the firefighters. The fire roared, its flames licking at the sky and devouring the building. Black smoke poured from the windows and rooftop, hanging over the structure like a death shroud.

A wave of nausea rolled over her.

Jax will be fine. This is what he does.

He'd told her himself they'd have to clear the entire building. That would take time.

Only time wasn't on their side. What if the roof collapsed?

No. She would not think like that. Better to stay busy than let doubt and fear creep in.

Bringing her camera up, she focused the lens on the upper floors of the building, searching for signs of life.

26

JAX

Jax climbed the stairs, thoughts of Becca derailing his concentration. Had she listened, for once, and stayed with the apparatus? The thought of her getting too close to the building, with smoke and debris flying, sliced at his gut.

Focus, asshole.

Distraction was a surefire way to get himself or one of his men hurt. He'd just have to trust that Becca was safe on the ground and behind the fire line where she belonged.

He made his way down the fourth-floor corridor, checking all the doors, with Smith at his heels.

"FDNY. Is there anyone in need of assistance?"

A strangled cry came from the end of the hall. Both men ran forward, stopping at the last door.

He checked the temperature before signaling Smith to break it down.

They'd cleared floors two and three already. He was trying not to think about the first floor, which had been fully engulfed when they arrived.

He hoped like hell the occupants had gotten out, but there

was nothing he could do for them now. They needed to focus on the lives they could still save.

Smith took an ax to the doorframe, striking close to the lock.

Sweat dripped down his face. They were running out of time. Flames licked at the stairwell, creeping toward them. "No freelancing. We make the grab and get out."

Smith nodded his understanding. Then, holding the ax to his chest, Smith kicked in the door.

Black smoke billowed out. Not a good sign.

Jax led the way. "Hello? FDNY. We're here to get you out."

No answer.

They quickly cleared the front rooms, inching down the narrow hall to the bedrooms.

The floorboards creaked beneath their feet.

"She's not going to hold much longer," Smith called, pushing open a bedroom door and scanning the room. "Clear."

Jax moved to the next door, which was closed. He pounded on the door. "FDNY!"

"We're in here." There was a loud sob. "Please help us."

"We're going to get you out," he called, trying the knob and finding it locked. "I need you to open the door for me."

A moment later, the door opened, revealing a young family inside. A mother and two small children. Their faces were stained with tears.

"Don't be afraid. We're going to take good care of you." He grabbed a stack of towels from the rack next to the sink and instructed them all to cover their mouths to prevent smoke inhalation. Then he turned to his partner. "Get them to the front room."

He picked up the first boy and handed him to Smith, directing the mother to follow. The second boy, he lifted in his own arms. The group hurried to the front bedroom, only to find the window painted shut.

"It's stuck," Smith hollered, waving them back. "I'm going to have to break it."

"Do it."

Two minutes and one death defying trip down the ladder later, they were all on the ground and the building was cleared.

When he peeled off his helmet and looked toward the apparatus, Becca was there, camera raised, focused on the family they'd just pulled out. She was engrossed in her work, dark hair blowing on the breeze. Their eyes met, and if he didn't know better, he'd have sworn it was relief that flooded her features as she nodded her acknowledgment.

Had she actually been worried about him?

He glanced at the burning building. During his time on the job, he'd seen much worse, but this one wasn't pretty. Wiping his face, he signaled for a paramedic to check on the children and clear them of smoke inhalation.

An hour later, when the fire was finally extinguished and the scene was clear, he found Becca sitting on the curb. "So what did you think of your first day on the job?"

"It was...I don't even know what to say. I can definitely see why they call you New York's Bravest." She drew her knees to her chest and wrapped her arms around them, watching the guys pack up their ladders. The engine company was rolling their hoses, a less than enviable task. "What's it like to run into a fire when everyone else is running out? To know you've made a difference, saved a life?"

He shrugged. No matter how many times he was asked that question, he didn't think he'd ever have an adequate answer. It wasn't that he was fearless; he just refused to let that fear control him.

Instead, he channeled it into action, saving the ones he could.

"Can I see?" he asked, pointing at the camera. She handed it over without protest, letting him flip through the pictures she'd taken. They were incredible. The angles. The light. The emotion. She was really talented. He'd expected as much, but seeing it firsthand through the lens of her camera? "These are really good," he said, returning the camera. "Erin is going to be very pleased."

"Don't change the subject." She looked at him, awestruck, her dark eyes shining with adoration he didn't deserve. "What you did today was amazing. I don't think I breathed the entire time you were in the building. Hell, my hands were shaking so bad it's a wonder I got any decent photos."

Her words landed like a sledgehammer to the gut.

Aside from his crew, there'd never been anyone in his life to give a damn about his safety.

"It's the job," he said, shoving the realization aside and slinging an arm across her shoulders. For once, she didn't protest. "Ask any guy here and you'll get the same answer. These guys aren't on the job for accolades and badge bunnies. They're on the job because it's in their blood. It's a family tradition, or a calling, or the only thing they've ever wanted to do."

"It's just so dangerous," she said, twisting to look at her shoulder where his hand rested. "And dirty."

"If you think that's dirty," he said, glancing at her blouse and realizing he'd smudged it with soot. "You don't know the meaning of the word."

Her lips curved, revealing her teeth. "And you're going to teach me?"

He squeezed her shoulder, remembering how she'd almost kissed him back at the firehouse.

Maybe this ride along wasn't such a bad idea after all. "Shortie, it would be my pleasure. And yours."

27

———

BECCA

BECCA SLIPPED ON HER SNEAKERS, promising herself that day two of the ride along would be free of sexual tension.

No almost kisses. No handholding. No dirty jokes.

No matter how good Jax looks covered in soot and sweat.

That was the problem, wasn't it?

His job was inherently sexy, requiring strength, loyalty, and bravery. Add to that mix the extreme arousal she got seeing him running into a burning building, and yeah, her resolve was melting fast.

The man was hot on her tail, and the more she got to know him, the harder it was to find excuses to resist. He wasn't nearly as big of an ass as she'd originally thought—okay, he wasn't an ass at all—and everything she'd seen of him seemed to prove he wasn't the same boy who'd bolted on her at sixteen.

And then there was the sex...

Shake it off, Mancini. You cannot let him back in your bed, no matter how big his apparatus is!

They were in the home stretch now.

She just had to get through the day with her panties intact, and then she could go back to her day job, sitting behind a desk, smiling and writing press releases for Garden of Dreams.

Only she wasn't nearly as excited by the prospect as she'd expected.

While the fire was devastating, she'd enjoyed being in the field, being in the thick of the action. That was her dream. In a city that never slept, there were always stories to tell.

She wanted to be the one to tell them.

Then quit being such a scaredy-cat and show your work. That's the only way to make your dream a reality. If you want it, go get it.

She sighed, hating it when the little voice in her head was right.

It was time to get over the debilitating case of rejectionitis she'd developed and take a chance on herself. Not everyone was going to like her work, and that was okay. The new piece she was finishing was good, both compositionally and artistically.

But was it good enough?

Only one way to find out. Pick ten galleries and submit.

Ten chances for rejection. Ten chances for success.

Feeling good about her decision, she was ready to tackle another day at the One-Three-Two.

The morning passed in a blur.

The company was holding a community open house and the firehouse was full to bursting with visitors. She'd taken hundreds of pictures, watching the day unfold through the lens of her camera. She'd learned quite a bit, too. Like many of the guys, including Jax, were Child Passenger Safety Technicians, certified to instruct and assist parents with proper car seat installation.

There had also been a steady stream of future firefighters making their way through the firehouse, eyes shining bright as they wiggled into the oversize turnout gear and climbed on the truck. She'd gotten some really great shots, so many that she'd be glued to her computer for days going through them and making edits.

It had also become quite apparent Jax wasn't kidding when he joked about badge bunnies.

No less than a dozen single women had shown up offering baked goods and requesting a tour of the firehouse. And the way they threw themselves at the single guys? Constantly touching their arms and giggling like schoolgirls?

It was ridiculous. And insulting.

Jealous much?

No. She was most definitely *not* jealous.

What did she have to be jealous of? Jax was a free man. Just because they'd had sex—the sensual, life-changing kind—didn't mean she had a claim on him.

Nor did she want one.

Jax strolled by with a plate of brownies. He paused, backing up a step. "Hungry? You should try one before they're gone. These things are like crack," he whispered, pulling one off the plate and popping it in his mouth whole.

A chocolate crumb clung to the corner of his lips as he chewed.

"More treats from your admirers?" She pushed the plate away. No matter how good they looked, she was definitely *not* eating those brownies. "I'll pass."

"Since when do you say no to chocolate?" He narrowed his eyes. "Wait a minute. You're not jealous, are you?"

"Of brownies?" she asked, tilting her head and playing dumb.

Judging by the shit-eating grin on his face, he wasn't buying her routine. "If I remember correctly, it wasn't so long ago you brought me a box of cookies just like this."

"That was different," she argued, wiping the stupid brownie crumb from his lip and cursing the way her belly fluttered when she touched him. So much for the whole "no touching" thing.

His blue eyes danced with laughter. "Oh, really?"

"I was trying to bribe you," she explained, lifting her chin. "Not seduce you. Or rather, half the firehouse."

"And here I thought it was a thank-you." He retreated, taking those blasted brownies with him. "Have it your way. But for the record? There's only one woman who can seduce me, and she sure as shit doesn't need a plate of brownies to do it." He winked at her. "Just say the word and I'm yours, Becca."

Well, crap. That totally backfired. How did he manage to make everything, even baked goods, sexy?

It was a gift, she'd give him that, because her pulse was pounding and her lips ached to be kissed.

Fifteen hours to go. Hang tough, Mancini.

When the station finally cleared out and the cleanup was done, she was thrilled to sit down for a hot meal and rest her feet. O'Rourke was serving up slow cooked ribs, and the smell of barbeque had her mouth watering, literally. Following the guys through the buffet line, she piled her plate high with salad and ribs before taking a seat at the far end of the table.

Just as her butt hit the chair, the alarm went off.

So much for resting my aching feet.

Four minutes and a whole lot of hustle later they arrived at the scene of a nasty collision.

Her stomach dropped as she climbed out of the truck.

A tiny Honda, not unlike her own, had been T-boned by a much larger SUV. Both cars appeared to be totaled, the subcompact smashed between the larger vehicle and a light pole. There was glass everywhere, and the driver of the car was slumped over the wheel, the horn blaring.

Standing clear of the emergency personnel, she began shooting the scene.

The driver of the SUV had walked away from the accident unharmed and stood watching, a look of shock etched on his face.

According to bystanders, he'd run the light, hitting the smaller car and losing control.

She pushed her personal feelings aside. There would be time for introspection and grief later.

The paramedics tried the doors on the smaller car, finding them inoperable. The driver was trapped, unconscious, and in need of medical attention. There was a teenage girl in the backseat, who thankfully, had been spared any serious harm.

The crew pulled out the back window and the crying girl crawled to safety.

She was hysterical, refusing to leave her mother's side, even for medical attention.

Becca shut off her camera.

She spent a lot of time with kids in her day job at Garden of Dreams. There was more she could do to help than just tell the story today, even if that meant being a shoulder to lean on and a voice of reassurance.

Capturing real life was important, but being human meant more.

28

JAX

Jax and Anderson assessed the damage to the driver's side door. It was extensive. No way in hell that door was coming open without hydraulic assistance. They just needed to determine the quickest attack plan. The paramedics had administered emergency care via the broken window, but the driver was in bad shape. The kind of care she needed wasn't available on the side of the road.

Every minute counted in a situation like this one.

"Engine block's intact," Anderson said. "We take the door, we'll have her out in no time."

"Agreed. Let's get the Jaws of Life in here and get to work."

He stepped aside to let the paramedic check her vitals again, confirming she hadn't regained consciousness. They'd staunched the bleeding, but who knew what kind of internal damage they were dealing with. They needed to be careful pulling her out.

Even with a collar and a longboard, they could cause additional damage. That was the last thing he wanted.

He had enough shit weighing on his conscience.

Anderson returned with the hydraulic tool and positioned it to cut through the steel door, starting at the top.

"Let's move," Jax said, glancing first at the vic and then her daughter, who was sitting on the curb, holding Becca's hand. He hated scenes like this. It was bad enough there was a life on the line, but her kid was watching. Sweat trickled down his brow. His heart was beating double time. Hell, he felt like he was going to need oxygen to get through the next hour. But this was the job. This was what they trained for, and they would not fail. *He would not fail.* "Clock's ticking. We are not going to lose her."

Thirty-five painstaking minutes later, they'd removed the door and loaded the driver on a bus to Brooklyn Hospital. Happy to make the handoff to the paramedics, he wiped the back of his hand across his forehead, studying the mangled car.

Some days the job was fucking hard.

They were expected to provide miracles, someway, somehow.

They saw the best and the worst of humanity. And the bad shit? That stuff ate at you day after day, night after night.

But when you had a good day?

It was a high like no other. And you held onto it like a lifeline, knowing it would pull you through hard times.

Today was a good day. They'd saved a life.

He watched as Becca helped the kid into the back of the ambulance. She'd been so cool under pressure, something he hadn't expected. Not everyone could handle the things emergency services faced.

Even more impressive was the fact that she'd put her camera down, forgoing the job she'd been paid to do in order to do the right thing.

In his line of work, he'd come across a lot of jaded assholes who put the job first, forgetting what mattered most. Maybe he shouldn't have been surprised— the Becca he'd known as a kid had always been empathetic toward others. It just wasn't a side of herself she'd shown much since he'd moved back to town.

Maybe because she was so damn busy trying to push him away.

Too bad it wasn't working.

She'd tipped her hand earlier with the brownies, revealing she cared more than she let on.

Little did she know they were from a happily married woman who'd just wanted to say thank you for giving her son a tour of the firehouse. He'd almost corrected Becca's assumption, but since she seemed determined to play coy, he'd thought, what the hell?

Two could play at that game.

No, she definitely hadn't scared him off. If anything, the last two days had convinced him not to give up on them, because whether she realized it or not, they had something real. Something that could be great if she'd let go of the past and give it a chance.

29

BECCA

Becca drove home from the firehouse feeling drained and edgy and frustrated. She hadn't slept well. Too much action, too much adrenaline, and apparently, too much pent-up sexual frustration. Her skin felt tight, restrictive, like she'd outgrown it entirely over the last few weeks.

Had she changed so much in such a short time?

Glancing in the rearview mirror, she confirmed Jax was following her. Determined to ensure she got home safe and sound, he'd insisted on it. He'd also told her she just had to say the word if she wanted him back in her bed, an offer that was sounding better with each passing block.

God help her, she was weak. And tired. Tired of fighting her attraction to him.

Because in just a few short weeks he'd claimed her in a way no other man could.

Every cell in her body reacted when he was near, coming alive and demanding ecstasy.

Pulling up to the curb, she threw the car in park and killed the engine.

She had the day off. She could go upstairs and let her little battery-operated friend do the job, but the fact was, it couldn't compare to the orgasms Jax offered. And if she was going to be thinking about Jax the whole time anyway, she might as well have him buried between her thighs.

Damn straight.

Decision made, she climbed out of the car and approached his SUV, pulling the driver's side door open. It was going to be a tight fit.

"Slide your seat back," she said, stepping up on the running board.

He raised a brow, but said nothing as he complied. The speed with which he followed her command was exhilarating. It also gave her room to climb into his lap, modesty be damned.

It was still early and the street was clear, absolving her of embarrassment.

Straddling him, she drank in his smoky scent, the look of surprise on his face, and the feel of his growing erection against her body. She crushed her mouth to his, parting his lips and swallowing the groan that rolled off his tongue.

"Jesus, Becca. What're you doing?" he panted as she ground her hips against his, relishing the feel of his hardened cock between her legs

God, her panties were so wet. She needed this. Needed him. *Now.*

Whatever control she had, she'd exhausted it.

This thing between them? It was burning hot and fast and hard.

"Isn't it obvious?" she asked, kissing her way down his neck. "I'm seducing you. I need you, Jax. I need you to come upstairs and fuck me. In the bed. On the table. In the shower. Whatever you want. I'm yours."

"Mine?" he asked, eyes growing dark. "I like the sound of that." He slipped his hand between her legs, rubbing her through her leggings. She responded instantly, her back arching to grant him better access. "But you should know the first rule of being my woman is that I don't like to share. I want you all to myself," he said, his voice a husky rasp as he rubbed her clit in slow, lazy circles. "That means I'm going to take you upstairs and fuck you right, where the only man who gets to see that beautiful body of yours is me."

She ravaged his lips, savoring the clean taste of mouthwash on his breath. "What are you waiting for, big guy?"

"Damn right, I'm big," he responded with a cocky grin. Then he opened the door and they spilled out into the street, joined at the lips.

Grabbing his hand, she pulled him toward the building, doing a mental happy dance when she discovered the elevator was back in service. She punched the call button and waited impatiently, shifting her weight from one foot to the other in a pointless attempt to relieve the achy need between her legs.

Jax lowered his lips to her ear, gently pushing her hair out of the way. "Don't worry." His tongue traced the curve of her ear. "I'll be inside you soon enough."

Hot. Damn.

She nearly came on the spot. Her panties had to be drenched. Never in her life had she needed a man so badly.

When the elevator door opened, she crashed into the guy from 5A in her haste to get inside. "Sorry."

She didn't look back, just pressed the button for the fifth floor.

The doors slid closed, and Jax cornered her, the hard lines of his body pinning her to the back wall of the elevator.

One of his hands snaked up her back. The other cupped her chin. "I've waited so long for this," he said, rubbing her cheek with the pad of his thumb, sending a shudder of desire to her limbs. "So long for you to say you need me like I need you. For you to say you're my woman."

Had she said those words? She hadn't meant to, but hell, she couldn't take them back now.

Clearly lust had short-circuited her brain.

Whatever. They could sort it out later.

Right now, the only thing she cared about was relieving the tension that had her body strung tight.

More like strung out.

Staring into her eyes, he pressed his erection to her stomach, rotating his hips and sending white-hot need searing through her body. Was he trying to kill her?

"Do you see what you do to me?" Her knees grew weak at his touch, lust pooling in her belly. "How hard you make me, Becca? No other woman can do that. Just you."

The elevator door slid open, and she bolted for her apartment.

With shaky hands, she reached for her keys, and after her two failed attempts at opening the deadbolt, Jax commandeered the key ring.

How was it he had complete control of his body when hers was spiraling out of control?

He opened the door, holding it wide for her to pass, but once that door closed, whatever careful control he'd constructed dissolved. Gone was the calm, collected man who'd performed miracles over the last two days, the one who kept it together when everything else was falling apart. He was voracious, lifting her from her feet and slamming her back against the wall, using his own arm to soften the impact as he lavished kisses upon her body. She wrapped her legs around him, locking her arms around his neck as he pumped his hips against hers.

She'd never experienced anything like it.

Never had a man been so hungry, so desperate—*for her.*

Using her legs for leverage, she slid up and down the length of his erection, enjoying the way he groaned against her neck and buried his face in her hair. When he brought his lips to her throat and sucked, she threw her head back, giving herself over to him, to the feel of his lips on her body, to the pleasure he offered.

It was too much. And not nearly enough.

They were burning up.

"We need to get rid of these clothes." He kissed her, gently this time, and set her on the floor. "Take off your clothes, Becca."

Kicking off her shoes, she stripped off her *Little Miss Sunshine* T-shirt and extended her arm, dropping the shirt at his feet. She slipped past him, letting her breasts brush against his arm in the process.

"Catch me if you can, big guy." Unhooking her bra, she swung it around and dropped it over her shoulder, revealing her hardened nipples. "I'll be naked and waiting—*for you.*"

Jax practically jumped out of his boots, but she didn't stick around to watch the rest.

Instead, she left a trail of clothing that stopped at the edge of the bed, where she lay stroking herself.

She was so close to coming, the tension in her body climbing to a crescendo. It wouldn't take much to push her over the edge, but she wanted—needed—it to be Jax who sent her flying.

He stepped into the bedroom, standing tall, oozing sex and confidence and a total lack of control. Kneeling at the end of the bed, he pushed her knees wide. "I want to see you," he ordered. "All of you."

Slowly, she withdrew her hand, letting him gaze upon her.

He grabbed her wrist, bringing her fingers to his mouth. Then he licked them, sucking her pointer finger into his mouth and taking it deep.

"You taste so damn good." He stroked her thighs, sending a shiver up her spine. "But I need more. So much more."

He lowered himself, settling between her legs, and licked her, his tongue a slow drag across her slick flesh. She closed her eyes, fisting her hands in the blankets and fighting to keep her orgasm at bay. She had no idea how she was going to do it, but she'd sure as hell try.

For him. *For Jax.*

They were just getting started. She didn't want it to end.

Not yet.

"Look at me, Becca." She propped herself up on her elbows, eyes meeting his. "I want to see the look on your face when you're screaming my name."

"Liar," she challenged, with a crooked grin. "You want to make sure I know who it is that makes me feel so good."

When he lowered his mouth to her again, his tongue massaging her in deliriously perfect ways, a sob wrenched from her lips. Her hips bucked off the mattress. "I can't take it, Jax. It's too much."

He looked at her with fierce determination. "You can, and you will."

Then he resumed his exploration, slipping his tongue inside of her and sucking hard.

Stars exploded behind her eyelids, and she wove her fingers through his hair, seeking purchase as her muscles contracted with ecstasy. He worked her until the last shudder, wringing every last drop of pleasure from her body.

Then he kissed her, slow and deep, his hands skimming over her hips, sending aftershocks to her boneless limbs. He stretched out next to her, his erection teasing her as it nudged her belly.

"Have I told you," he asked, sucking on her neck, "that you have..." He moved south, licking her nipple and sucking it into his mouth. His tongue skated across the peak, sending a fresh wave of arousal crashing through her. "The most..." His lips crept lower, creating a trail down her abdomen. "Amazing body."

He plunged a finger inside of her, and she cried out, needing more.

She'd never had two orgasms before, but she had a feeling Jax would have no problem delivering. "Condoms are in the nightstand."

He opened the drawer and paused.

Blood rushed to her cheeks.

"You like toys?" he asked, holding up her hot pink vibrator. "I'll keep that in mind. But today? You're all mine."

He replaced the vibrator and grabbed a condom, tearing open the foil wrapper and rolling it over his length.

He buried himself deep on the first stroke, filling her completely. His body tensed, the muscles in his back rippling under her fingers. "You feel so damn good."

She wrapped her legs around him, loving the way they fit together so perfectly. "Don't hold back."

His lips collided with hers, kissing her hard and fast in concert with his thrusts. Their hips crashed together in harmony, both moving toward the explosive grand finale. When he threw his head back, calling her name, she was right there with him, her body racked by her own shattering release.

30

JAX

Jax woke with a start, and checked his watch. It was just after noon. He rolled over, finding the other side of the bed empty.

No surprise there. It was exactly why he hadn't meant to fall asleep.

He'd just been so damn tired. And having Becca wrapped in his arms in that big comfy bed, after two nights at the station?

It was bound to happen.

Throwing back the covers, he climbed out of bed and began searching for his clothes before remembering they were in the living room. Good thing he wasn't shy. He padded down the hall and found Becca in the tiny kitchen.

"I'm making omelets," she called over her shoulder. "They're almost ready." She turned around, her eyes going straight to his cock. "And apparently so are you."

"Don't worry. I'll let you eat first." He scooped up his clothes, keeping his eyes fixed on the tiny robe she wore. It was short, thin, and sexy. "After? I make no promises."

"Duly noted," she said, waving her spatula and returning her attention to the cooktop.

He watched her work, knowing their next conversation

would set the tone for...whatever it was they were doing. She hadn't kicked him out yet, and that was a damn good sign. He didn't want to push too hard, but he also didn't want to go back to the way things were before. In the time they'd spent together at the station, they'd made a real breakthrough.

Maybe it was time for another.

"Here you go," she said, dropping a plate and fork in front of him at the bar.

She pulled a quart of juice from the fridge and poured them each a glass before joining him.

They ate in silence, each of them presumably lost in thought. If it had been anyone else, he'd have been twitching, but it wasn't awkward. In fact, it was comfortable, as if they didn't need words to fill the space between them.

When they were finished, she reached for his plate.

"Wait," he said, taking her hand. "There's something I wanted to ask you."

"Sure." Her smile faltered. "What's up?"

"I wanted to see if you had plans Saturday night?" Hoping to set her at ease, he smiled. "I'd like to take you on a real date."

"Jax," she said, doubt clouding her eyes. "I don't think that's a good idea."

"Really?" he asked, refusing to give up on her. "Because we've tried staying apart, and that hasn't exactly worked. For either one of us."

She chewed her bottom lip.

"Look, Becca. I came back to Brooklyn to find you and make things right. Not because of some misguided teenage guilt, but because I've never *ever* connected with anyone the way I connected with you. Nothing you say or do is going to make me feel differently."

"We fight all the time," she said, tucking her hair behind her ear with her free hand.

"Fighting, foreplay." He squeezed her hand, looking her square in the eye. "Tomato, tomahto. You can keep on trying to push me away, but it's not going to work. I'm not the same kid I was before. I'm a different man, and I'm going to do whatever it takes to prove it to you. You can trust me. I will never *ever* hurt you like that again."

"I want to believe you," she said, rubbing her forehead. "I just...I don't know."

"One date," he said, holding up a finger to emphasize the singularity of the proposal. If it went well, and he had every confidence it would, he'd worry about date number two. Baby steps beat rejection all day long. "Give me one date, Becca Mancini."

"Okay. One date." She flashed him a challenging smile without a trace of doubt. "You've got one date, Jackson Hart.

Better make it count."

31

BECCA

BECCA STRIPPED off her halter top and tossed it on the mountain of clothes covering her bed. She eyed the discarded shirts. None of them felt right for her first date with Jax.

Which was ridiculous.

Clearly he didn't give a damn what she wore, or even, based on their tryst at the warehouse, if it was clean.

She sighed and trudged back into the closet, the butterflies in her stomach rioting angrily.

Just pick something already. Close your eyes if you have to, but for the love of God, just pick something. Two dates from now, it won't even matter.

After all, a three-date max was her MO. But calling it quits with Jax?

The very thought of it made her queasy.

He definitely wouldn't make it easy for her. The man had made it quite clear he wouldn't go down without a fight.

On the other hand, the idea of anything more scared the crap out of her.

With her photography business coming together, the last

thing she needed to be worried about was nursing a broken heart. Been there, done that, have the scars to prove it.

Quit overthinking. It's one date. One. No big deal.

The buzzer sounded.

Shit.

She pulled a black-and-white striped tank from the hanger and tugged it over her head, slipping her feet into a pair of red ballet flats. It would have to be good enough.

Clutching her purse, she hightailed it downstairs, stopping at the intercom to let her date know she was on the way down.

Her date.

Talk about a strange turn of events. Never in a million years had she imagined Jackson Hart would ask for a second first date. Or that her answer would be yes.

At least he'd shown up this time.

Forgive and forget, remember?

Jax was waiting dutifully when she stepped out into the cool spring night.

"You look great." His eyes raked over her body, sending a flash of heat straight to her core.

"You don't look so bad yourself." Total understatement. He looked like walking sex in a pair of dark jeans and a black T-shirt that hugged his body like a second skin, emphasizing the drool-worthy perfection of his physique. "So where are we going?"

"Somewhere we should have gone a long time ago," he said, opening the passenger door with a smug grin. God, she loved those dimples. "I think you're going to like it."

Unable to weasel any more clues out of him, she climbed in and sat back, resigned to her fate. Wherever they were going, she'd know soon enough.

He hopped on Ocean Parkway and drove south.

"How's the new piece coming?" he asked, glancing over and turning the radio down. "Ready for consumption yet?"

"I should know in a couple of weeks," she admitted, twisting the hem of her shirt. "I think it's ready, but that's really up to the professionals. I submitted it to ten galleries for consideration."

"That's amazing." He covered her hands with one of his own. "I don't imagine it's easy waiting for a decision."

She forced a laugh. "I swear I'm so nervous, I can hardly function. I've been checking my email obsessively for a reply."

"Does the piece have a name?" he asked.

"I'm calling it Corner View." She chewed her bottom lip. "I wasn't sure at first, but the more I worked on it, the more I realized the city means something different to each of us. The people, the places, the dreams. It wasn't just about capturing life, it was about capturing life through *my* lens."

He squeezed her hand. "I can't wait to see it."

Twenty-five minutes later, Jax turned onto Surf Avenue, finding an open parking spot on the street.

Coney Island.

Tension laced her muscles, and those damn butterflies started acting up again.

The date may have been ten years overdue, but her nerves hadn't gotten the message. They were on high alert, wreaking havoc with her body. She wiped her palms on her thighs.

Jax shut off the car and removed his seat belt, turning to face her.

"What are we doing?" She bit her lip. "Why did you bring me here?"

"I want a do-over." He touched her chin, sending a shiver of anticipation down her spine. Her breath caught in her throat. The look in his eyes was pure devotion, as if his very happiness depended on her answer. "I was an immature, selfish son of a bitch, and I don't deserve a second chance, but I'm asking for it anyway. I want to start fresh and do things right this time. I want to take you on the date we should've had ten years ago."

Well, crap. What could she say to that? It was the sweetest damn thing any man had ever said to her, and her ovaries wholeheartedly agreed. But he was wrong. He *did* deserve a second chance. They both did.

Why had it taken her so long to see that?

Because you're a stubborn ass. Obviously.

"What do you say?" he asked, his face hopeful.

"I say…" She drew a steadying breath, praying she wouldn't go down in flames. "I've always wanted to make out on the Wonder Wheel."

He leaned forward, brushing a feather light kiss on her lips. "I think we can make that happen."

They walked through the park hand in hand, bypassing the carousel and heading straight for the fifteen-story tall wheel. The lights and sounds of the park were just as she remembered them from her childhood: loud, colorful, and completely Coney Island. She drank in the briny sea air, letting it wash over her and calm her frayed nerves. It wasn't like she'd committed to anything more than making out on the Wonder Wheel like a couple of teenagers.

Besides, Jax wouldn't hurt her. Not again.

She wouldn't let him.

But what if he'd actually changed?

She sneaked a peek at him, loving the cool confidence that rolled off him like a summer breeze.

While she was a ball of anxiety, he was perfectly at ease, as if he knew he'd planned the perfect date. Sweet. Romantic. Symbolic. Warmth spread through her body, fanning out from her belly. When he'd asked for a do-over, it hadn't occurred to her he meant it quite so literally.

Jax bypassed the open sliding car and chose a stationary one when it was their turn to board. He held the door and let her climb in first.

"No swinging?" she asked, scooting across the ancient metal bench. "You're not afraid, are you?"

"You do know this thing is like ninety-years-old right?" He draped an arm over her shoulder, the weight a comforting presence on the terrifyingly ancient ride. "You're crazy if you're not scared. Besides, the only distraction I need is you."

A familiar tension coiled low in her belly, reminding her just how badly she wanted Jackson Hart.

How badly she'd always wanted him.

The wheel began to move, lifting their car into the air. A few more passengers were loaded, elevating them enough to see the ocean. Waves lapped at the shoreline, barely audible over the cacophony of noise coming from the amusement park.

Jax rubbed her thigh with his free hand, his fingers digging deep as he massaged the soft tissue, setting her nerves on fire. No wonder he was so good at his job. The man had a talent for locating hot spots.

Their car paused at the pinnacle of the ride, one hundred and fifty feet in the air, giving them a panoramic view of the beach. Although it was a clear night, the lights of the boardwalk left the stars muted against the inky night sky.

"Look. You can see the Brooklyn Bridge. It's beautiful," she breathed, trying not to let him see how affected she was by his touch.

Oh, who are you kidding? Odds are, he already knows.

"The view is nice," he agreed, moving his hand from her thigh to her chin. "But it's not half as beautiful as you."

His lips descended upon hers with urgency, nipping and sucking with a gentleness he'd never shown before.

The kisses were soft and sweet. Chaste almost. Like a first kiss.

It was exactly how she'd imagined her first date with Jax would be.

The ride began to move again, this time bypassing the busy loading deck and completing a full rotation. She didn't care. There was only one thing she wanted—one thing she needed—and Jax was delivering, his kisses growing wilder and more passionate, like a fire blazing out of control.

She breathed in his scent, memorizing every perfect moment as his lips moved over hers, never breaking contact as the wheel spun round and round. When it finally stopped and the operator opened their car door, her cheeks were flushed, a telltale sign she'd been thoroughly kissed and loved every second of it.

They exited the ride, and Jax grabbed her hand, pulling her body flush to his, her breasts crushed against his chest. Tucking a loose strand of hair behind her ear, he smoothed her wild curls. It was a pointless endeavor.

It was also not the point.

The way he was looking at her? With unabashed hunger in his eyes?

She was his for the taking.

He could ask for anything, and she'd be powerless to refuse him.

Despite all the bickering and banter, despite her best efforts to extinguish this thing between them, she was falling for him.

Again.

No one had ever made her feel the way he did. Off kilter. Excited. Special.

Like she'd been made for him alone.

"So what did you think of the Wonder Wheel?" he asked.

"It was everything I expected. And more." Stretching up on her toes, she fused her lips with his, giving him a not so PG-13 kiss. "Wanna go down to the beach?"

"Oh, no you don't." He separated their molded bodies and swatted her on the ass. "This is our first date. You're not going to lure me down to the beach and take advantage of me." He took her hand, giving it a squeeze. "Not yet, anyway."

She stuck out her tongue. "Spoilsport."

"What kind of man do you think I am?" he asked, feigning indignation. She arched her brow, letting him know *exactly* what kind of man she thought he was. "On second thought, don't answer that. At least not until I've proven my masculine prowess by winning you a carnival teddy bear."

"A carnival teddy bear, huh?" A grin tugged at her lips. "How very manly and romantic."

"It's tradition," he reminded her, leading the way to a water game that promised a winner every time. "Besides, I have a strategy."

"A guaranteed win?" she teased, pointing at the sign.

He scoffed and puffed out his chest. "Stick to what I know. All you have to do is spray the target in the clown's mouth to inflate the balloon on its head. First one to inflate their balloon wins." He slapped a ten-dollar bill down on the counter and took a seat next to a couple of kids. "How hard can it be? This is what I do."

She covered her mouth, stifling her laughter. "You're right. You definitely have an advantage."

The cashier took his money and quickly made change for everyone at the counter. Then she sounded the alarm and five streams of water shot across the booth.

Jax was right on target, his balloon inflating slow and steady. She glanced down the line, noticing the boy at the end had a slight advantage. His balloon seemed to be inflating at a faster rate. She swung her gaze back to Jax, smiling at the look of concentration on his face. It wasn't quite as intense as she'd seem him on the job, but he looked pretty damn determined to win that bear.

Pop!

The boy at the end of the counter broke out in a celebratory cheer, and Jax groaned, realizing he'd lost to a ten-year-old.

"You do know I'm going to have to play again, right?" He raked a hand through his hair, as if his man card really were in jeopardy. "I'm not leaving without one of those pink, fluffy bears."

The kids climbed down, and she took the empty seat next to him. "Looks fun. I'd like to give it a try."

He paid the cashier as a new group of players joined them at the counter.

Becca positioned herself, ensuring she was on target and waited for the buzzer to sound.

It had been years since she'd played a game like this, but if she was playing, she meant to win.

"Good luck." She nudged Jax with her foot. "You're going to need it."

"The lady has a competitive streak." He studied her, brows knit together. "Just so you know, I find that incredibly sexy. There are lots of games we can play, but I prefer the ones where we both win. Together."

Ignoring his attempt at distraction, she focused on her target, pressing down on the button that would release the water.

When the buzzer finally sounded, her stream sailed across the booth, missing the target. She adjusted quickly and watched the red balloon grow, rapidly increasing in size. It grew and grew and—*pop!*

She squealed with delight and chose the pinkest, fluffiest bear from the hanging prizes. Then she offered it to Jax, loving the horrified look on his face as he realized she'd won the bear for him.

"It's tradition," she reminded him, loving the blush that filled his cheeks.

It was about time she knocked him off balance.

Finally, he accepted the bear. "If the guys ever catch wind of this, I'll never live it down," he said, shaking his head in disbelief.

"Did you want to try again?" she asked, striving for innocence. "Third time's the charm."

"Shortie, I know when to admit defeat." He slid an arm around her waist. "And in case you haven't noticed, I already have the prize."

32

JAX

Jax walked Becca to her door, hardly able to believe how well the date had gone.

Hell, it had gone better than he could have imagined.

He just hoped she could see he was serious about a fresh start. And a real relationship with her.

They'd had an amazing evening at Coney Island.

After leaving the amusement park, they'd shared a pizza at Grimaldi's and taken a moonlit walk on the beach. It was sweet and romantic and everything their first date should have been. Even if he had failed in his mission to win her a stuffed bear.

He hadn't minded that she beat him.

The way her eyes lit up when she claimed victory had been worth it. His ego wasn't so overblown he couldn't handle losing to a woman.

His woman.

Becca Mancini was his woman. She didn't know it yet, but she would soon enough.

He grinned. And when she finally realized it? That would be the real flash point.

She stopped at her front door and spun around.

Raising her lips to his, she kissed him and slid her hand under the hem of his T-shirt. White-hot need raced straight to his cock.

"Why don't you come in for a drink?" she whispered.

Using every last ounce of control he possessed, he removed her hand from his abs. He needed to stick to the plan, which would be impossible if she kept stroking him like that. "Not tonight."

"Not tonight?" She frowned, her face falling. "You do know I was actually talking about sex, right?"

He brushed her cheek, his fingers finding their way to her tangled curls. Then, using his body, he backed her up to the door, pinning her with his larger frame. She looked up at him from under impossibly long lashes, her eyes growing dark.

"We're not going to have sex on our first date," he explained, rubbing his thumb across her lower lip. She trembled, lip quivering under his touch. "Or our second. Or even our third."

She opened her mouth to protest, but he shut her down, ravaging her lips.

He poured every last bit of need he had into the kiss, his tongue skating over hers seductively as his hardened cock pressed against her belly, a sharp contrast to her softness.

Damn. He needed her all right. But no matter how bad he wanted to bury himself between her thighs and make her moan with pleasure, he couldn't do it.

Not tonight. Not until she knew beyond a shadow of a doubt that she was his woman.

Then? All bets were off.

He'd have her every way she'd let him and enjoy every sinful second of it.

"We're not going to have sex until our fourth date," he explained, tilting her chin and forcing her to look him in the eye. "Do you know why that is, Becca?"

She swallowed, her throat bobbing slowly.

"Yeah, you know, don't you? You don't want to admit it, but deep down, in that hot, wet place, you know." He reached between her legs, stroking the very part of her body that ached for him. "Well, let me spell it out for you. You've never let any guy make it to the fourth date, have you? That's okay. I'm not just any guy. I'm the man who's going to break your three-date rule. I'm the one who knows every inch of your body and how to make it come apart with pleasure. I'm your man." He lowered his forehead to hers. "And you're my woman."

33

———

BECCA

Becca sat at her desk, staring at a blank monitor. She was supposed to be writing a press release for an upcoming charity event, but between the gallery submissions and Jax, her brain was otherwise occupied.

You're my woman.

Jax's words kept echoing through her brain.

Part of her rebelled against the idea. It was archaic. Restrictive. Neanderthal.

But the other part of her?

The part she'd thought no longer dreamed of fairytale romance? That part of her reveled at the idea of being Jackson Hart's woman, the thought infusing her with warmth that wrapped around her like a silk blanket.

His woman.

The one he'd make love to on hot summer nights, the one he'd hold close to his heart and share his life with...*if* they could get past the fatal fourth date.

That was a big *if*.

She sighed. It was pointless. She was completely and utterly incapable of focusing.

Maybe she'd call Erin. They could meet up for an early lunch, and she could try the press release again later.

She pulled her cell phone from her purse and unlocked the screen.

One missed call.

Tapping the voicemail button, she brought the phone to her ear.

"Hello, this message is for Rebecca Mancini. My name is Madeline Shortt and I am one of the curators at 440 Gallery. I received your portfolio and would like to discuss your work. You can reach me at seven-one-eight—" She scrambled for a pen and a scrap of paper, heart racing, and jotted down the number. "I look forward to speaking with you."

The message ended, and she dropped the phone on the desk.

Holy. Crap.

She stared at the gallery number, hands shaking.

Should she call right away, or was that too desperate? Maybe it would be better to wait a few hours.

Oh, who cared? The suspense was killing her.

Collecting her thoughts, she picked up the phone and dialed.

Twenty head-spinning minutes later, she had an offer to show her work—in short order—at 440 Gallery. Another artist had pulled out, and she was in. Talk about good timing. Heart bursting with joy, she did a happy dance at her desk.

She needed to tell someone, to share the good news.

No, she needed to tell Jax. After all, he was the only one she'd even told about her submissions.

Hmm, I wonder why that is?

All right, I get it. No need for sarcasm.

She dialed his number, chewing her bottom lip as the phone rang.

"Hey, beautiful."

"Hey, yourself," she said, grinning from ear to ear. He seemed to have that effect on her lately. Talk about a turn of events. "You're never going to believe who just called me."

His laughter came across the line rich and smooth. "In that case, why don't you just tell me?"

"440 Gallery. They want to include my work in an upcoming exhibition." She squealed again, unable to contain her enthusiasm. "Can you believe it?"

"Can I believe it?" he asked. "After seeing the photos you took on the ride along? Definitely. They'd be crazy not to want you. Congratulations."

"Thanks," she said, resting her chin in her hand. "I just can't believe it's really happening. First the FDNY Calendar of Heroes and now an exhibition? It's like a dream come true."

"I have a feeling this will be the first of many Mancini shows," he returned, without hesitation. "Which means we need to celebrate. I'm taking you to dinner tonight."

"Tonight?" she asked, sitting up straight.

"Unless you have other plans?"

She quickly ticked off their dates in her head. There was the first night at Coney Island. Then he'd taken her to the Promenade for a picnic at sunset. And last week he'd asked her to the Whitney for a lesson in art appreciation.

Dammit. This date was unlucky number four. But she wanted to say yes. God, did she want to say yes.

So, say yes. What's the big deal?

The big deal? The words were lodged in her throat like a bowling ball.

This was a big freaking step. And they both knew it.

"Becca?" he asked quietly. "You still with me?"

"No," she blurted out, her belly churning anxiously. "I mean, no, I don't have any plans."

"So, yes to dinner?" he asked, his voice flooded with relief.

"Yes." Confidence surged through her body. This was right. She knew it in her bones, all the way down to her curled toes. A fourth date with Jax meant something akin to commitment. It also meant pleasure. "What time are you picking me up?"

34

JAX

JAX TUGGED at the collar of his shirt as he rode the elevator up to Becca's apartment. He hated dressing up, but this was a big day for her, and he wanted it to be special. Landing her first gallery exhibition was something she'd remember for the rest of her life. No matter how many shows she booked in the future, the first would always be the most memorable.

It was also their fourth date, which was a pretty big deal, too. For both of them.

He'd sensed her initial hesitation, but when she'd accepted, her decision had been firm. And damn if that hadn't given him the confidence to take the next step. He was going to ask her for a commitment. She wasn't dating anyone else, but he wanted to make it official, so she'd know how serious he was about their relationship.

Six months ago, the idea of asking a woman for something more would've caused him to break out in hives, but Becca was different. She was everything he wanted in a woman. Passionate, loyal, funny, driven, beautiful. And she understood him in a way no one else could, including his passion for the job.

He wanted more from her, and he wanted to *be* more for her.

The only way that could happen was if they had the guts to put their hearts on the line.

It wouldn't be easy, but dammit, they had to try. He wouldn't have it any other way.

Becca was waiting for him when he arrived at the fifth floor.

"You look incredible," he said, slipping an arm around her waist and kissing her neck. Dressed in a short white dress that complimented her olive complexion, and a pair of ankle boots, she looked good enough to eat. Hell, he was ready to skip right to dessert. "You smell good, too."

"Nice try, lover boy. I'm starving." She laughed and grabbed his hand, dragging him into the elevator. "Where are we eating?"

"Mancini's. I've been craving your mom's pasta all week."

What he didn't say was that her closest friends and family had gathered at the restaurant to celebrate the news of her exhibition.

When they stepped through the door to Mancini's, the restaurant broke out in a raucous round of applause and cheering. Becca turned first to him and then to the bar where a homemade "Congratulations, Frankie!" banner hung.

"Did you do this?" she asked, looking up at him with glassy eyes.

"As much as I'd like to keep you all to myself tonight, I thought you should share this moment with all the people you love most."

"Thank you," she said, bracing a hand against his chest.

"You're welcome." He lowered his mouth to her ear, his heart hammering beneath her palm. "Don't worry. I plan on taking you back to my place later to make up for lost time."

"I like the sound of that," she said, brushing a kiss across his lips for all her friends and family to see.

They spent the next couple of hours eating and drinking and stuffing themselves with dessert. It was the Mancini way, and he relished being part of it, watching Becca laugh and celebrate with those nearest and dearest to her.

"So, it's official, then?" Christopher asked, wiping down the bar and following Jax's gaze to his sister. "You two going together?"

"Not yet, but I'm working on it." Jax sipped his beer. "Ask me again tomorrow."

"Good luck, man." Chris poured a shot of whiskey and slid it across the bar. "You're like a brother to me, but she's blood. You hurt her, and you'll be answering to me."

Jax nodded and raised the whiskey to his lips. The alcohol burned a path to his belly, solidifying his resolve. "I'll take good care of her."

Chris slapped the bar and returned to his family, giving his sister a bear hug and kissing the top of her head.

"I'll take good care of her," he repeated, promising himself he would be true to his word.

He'd never hurt her, not again. Becca deserved the best, and somehow he'd find a way to be that man.

For her.

When the party finally wrapped up, and they'd closed down the restaurant, they headed back to his place. Although they'd both had plenty to drink, the conversation weighing on his mind was sobering. He hoped like hell she felt the same way he did.

Becca wandered through his apartment barefoot, admiring all the eclectic pieces he'd found to fill the small space. "You have good taste," she said, glancing over her shoulder at him as she dragged her fingers across the top of a refurbished buffet table.

She looked right at home under his roof, a thought that made his balls tight as he watched her sashay back down the hall, shaking her ass all the way.

The urge to possess her completely, in body, mind, and spirit, surged.

First things first. He grabbed a bottle of water and followed, finding her sitting on the bed.

"This is our fourth date." As if he could possibly forget. His restraint had been pushed to the limit over the last few weeks as she'd tried to convince him to ditch his four-dates before-sex rule. "You know what that means?"

Oh, he knew all right. His cock wouldn't let him forget. Nor would that short little skirt. He knew exactly what was underneath, and he wanted it bad.

But first they needed to talk.

Fuck.

Maybe his man card was at risk after all. Conversation before sex? The woman really did have him tied up in knots.

"Before we go any further, there's something I want to ask you." He sat on the bed next to her, twisting the top off the water bottle and offering it to her. "Are you in or are you out?"

She sipped the water, her eyes shifting around the room as if she might find the answer pinned to the wall.

"I'm all in, but I need to know if you feel the same way. I want it all with you, Becca. Not just a couple of dates and hot sex. I want the relationship, the labels, the commitment. All of it."

Her gaze settled on the dresser.

She set the water bottle on the nightstand and slipped off the bed, padding across the room. "What's this?" she asked, picking up the card on the dresser.

"You don't recognize it?" He stood and joined her, peering over her shoulder.

She opened the valentine, hands shaking, and read the inscription.

Love, Frankie.

"I wasn't even sure you ever got it." She placed the card back on the dresser with care and turned to him, curiosity lighting her eyes. "You never said anything."

"What could I say?" He shrugged, hating the way the conversation had turned to old wounds for both of them. "I knew I wasn't good enough for you, but I was determined to try. That's why it took me three months to ask you out. I wanted to prove to myself that I could be better—for you." He brushed his knuckles across her cheek, grounding himself in the present. "Unfortunately, my old man had different plans. After my mom passed, he wasn't...he was different. Difficult to live with, unpredictable, drank a lot. It was the reason we moved constantly."

"I'm so sorry, Jax." Tears threatened to spill from her eyes. His gut twisted. This wasn't going right. Not. At. All. She glanced at the card. "After all these years, you still have it. Why?"

He scrubbed a hand over his face.

The truth was a real bitch sometimes. He didn't want her pity, but she deserved the truth, no matter how bad it hurt him. "It was the only valentine I ever received from someone who actually cared about me, and who I cared about in return."

She nodded, as if she understood. Or maybe she didn't trust her voice.

Hell, the last thing he wanted to do was make her cry.

"This isn't about who we were before." He laced his fingers with hers. "It's about who we are now. I want to be with you and only you."

"I—" She glanced around helplessly. "That's—"

Lowering his mouth to hers, he silenced her with a kiss, his lips brushing hers softly.

With Becca, he'd found home, but he needed to know she felt it, too. "I know a commitment is a big step. It scares the hell out of me, too, but there's no one else I'd rather take this leap with. I'm falling for you, Becca. If you don't feel the same way—"

She grabbed his neck and pulled his mouth to hers, silencing him with her lips as they moved savagely over his. The woman tasted of red wine and chocolate, a delicious, erotic combination, but he needed an answer. They couldn't fuck their way out of this one.

"Becca—"

"I'm yours," she said, pressing her body to his as if to prove her point. "The relationship, the labels, the commitment. All of it," she breathed, unbuttoning his shirt. "I've always been yours. I just didn't know it until now."

Holy fuck.

He needed to be inside his woman now. His cock demanded it, demanded release in the wet heat of the only woman who'd ever had his heart. No more history. No more talking.

Unzipping her dress, he slipped the straps over her shoulders, letting it fall to the floor.

She wasn't wearing a bra, and those perfect tits were right there, her hardened nipples ready for him. He leaned down, teasing them with his tongue, first the left, then the right. Drawing the rosy bud into his mouth, he sucked on it, massaging it with his tongue.

She moaned, arching her back as if begging him to take her deeper into the warm recess of his mouth.

"You like that?" he asked, slipping his arm behind her back and supporting her weight. "There are so many things I could do to make you feel good. And tonight I'm going to do all of them."

"Just know I'm going to hold you to that." She unbuttoned his pants, stripping him of his jeans and boxers as she fell to her knees. Her tiny hand wrapped around the base of his cock. The sight of her on her knees, licking her lips, nearly undid him. "I've waited a long time for this."

He groaned. If she kept talking like that, he really would lose control.

Twisting his fingers in her hair, he lost himself in her touch, watching as her tongue darted out to lick the head of his cock. Her mouth was hot and wet, and tension coiled at the base of his spine as she swirled her tongue around the tip.

"That's right. Take me in your mouth. I need to feel those sweet lips wrapped around my cock."

She licked the length of him, obliterating coherent thought, and drew him into her mouth, sucking hard and taking him deep. His body tensed, and it was all he could do not to pump his hips into her mouth as she worked him with her tongue, moving him toward orgasm at light speed.

Shit. The sight of her fucking him with her mouth? After weeks without sex?

It was more than he could take.

"Jesus, Becca. I can't—"

No way was he going to come without her. He pulled out and grabbed her under the arms, lifting her onto the dresser.

"That mouth of yours feels too damn good." He pulled a condom out of the top drawer, tore it open, and rolled it on. "I need to be inside you."

She wrapped her legs around him, crushing her lips to his as he plunged into her. Hard and deep, just how she liked it. Her moan of pleasure drove him on as he kissed his way down her neck, loving the taste of her salty skin. He slipped an arm around her backside, holding her in place as their hips crashed together.

"Jax," she panted, her legs squeezing him tight. "I'm going to come."

"That's right." He pumped into her, driving them both toward release. "Come for me."

Her nails raked over his shoulder as she screamed out his

name, her body clenching him tight. Three strokes later, he joined her, his own orgasm searing through his cock like white lightning, electrifying his senses. He'd never experienced anything like it, riding that fine line between pleasure and pain, coming inside the woman he loved. Because he did love Becca. He'd been wrong when he said he was falling in love with her.

He was already gone.

35

BECCA

BECCA SCROLLED through the images from her ride along with Ladder One-Three-Two, tagging images that had merit for Erin's series. Since she'd taken hundreds of photos, it was best to narrow the pool before she began editing.

Otherwise, she'd lose her mind and more hours than she cared to count.

She stopped on an image from the apartment fire. Jax was descending the ladder with a small boy in his arms.

How had she missed this one before?

Zooming in on his face, she studied his eyes. The photo wasn't perfect from a technical perspective. The light was a little off and the angle could've been better, but the look in his eyes?

Sheer determination. It truly embodied the miracle of the human spirit.

She marveled again at his ability to do the job after losing his own mother to the flames. Facing every day the thing you feared most?

As far as she was concerned, that was the definition of courage.

It was also one of the traits that drew her to him like a raindrop to a puddle.

Despite his difficult upbringing, despite losing his mother, despite a father who didn't give a damn about him, he'd become an amazing man. One who was funny and thoughtful and brave. He was exactly the kind of man she'd always known he could be.

And he made her feel…sweet Jesus, he made her feel things she hadn't even known existed, things she couldn't put into words. But above all, he made her feel like she was *his*.

Now and always.

The idea terrified her and thrilled her all at the same time.

Being in a relationship with Jax was everything she'd never let herself dream of, and that scared the hell out of her. She'd long ago accepted that happily ever after wasn't for her. It was easier than opening herself up to heartache and despair again.

But now that it was within her grasp? She couldn't stop thinking about it.

Sure, her relationship with Jax had the potential for disaster written all over it, but what if it actually worked out?

She tagged the image and moved to the next, reminding herself to stay on task and not get sidetracked like a love-struck teenager. There would be plenty of time later to sort out her tumultuous feelings.

For now, she needed to remain focused and get through these edits, or Erin would have her ass.

Her phone buzzed. She glanced at it vibrating on the counter and decided to let it go to voicemail.

Whoever it was could wait. Erin was a stickler with deadlines, and she couldn't afford to be late.

Weeks had passed since the ride along, but with all the prep work for the exhibition, she hadn't gotten around to finishing the editing, and they were down to the wire.

Two minutes later, the phone buzzed again.

Sighing, she climbed from her chair and went to retrieve it.

Unknown number.

She swiped the screen and brought it to her ear, hoping it wasn't a telemarketer because she was so *not* in the mood.

"Hello?"

"May I please speak with Becca Mancini?" a harried voice asked.

"Speaking." She dropped back into her desk chair and moved to the next picture in the series. "Can I help you?"

"Yes. My name is Dr. Krishnan. I'm calling from New York Methodist Hospital." Fear blossomed in her chest, its icy tendrils spreading through her body. "I have a patient here, uh, Jackson Hart, who listed you as his emergency contact."

Oh, God. Jax.

Her stomach plummeted.

"Is he okay?" she asked, not giving a damn about common courtesy.

"He suffered a line of duty injury, but yes, he's fine," the doctor said. "He's been treated and can probably be released later this evening. He'll need someone to take him home and stay the night, though. He shouldn't be alone."

"Okay." She moved to the hall closet and grabbed a pair of sneakers. "You said New York Methodist, right?"

"Yes, he's in the ER. Just check in at the desk when you arrive and give them his name."

"Thank you." She disconnected and slipped her feet into the shoes, grabbing her purse on the way out the door and slinging it over her shoulder.

The drive to the hospital felt endless, her stomach churning the entire way as she crawled across town.

Do not hurl in the car. That is not going to help. Besides, the doctor said he was fine. Take a deep breath and calm down.

Calm down? Impossible. Her brain was imagining every horrific scenario.

She should've asked for more details.

Would the doctor have given them to her? Did being an emergency contact give her access to his medical care? And when had Jax made her his emergency contact, anyway?

No need to ask why he'd done it.

She knew that sad answer, and it broke her damn heart.

He didn't have anyone else. But that wasn't really true. Not anymore.

The Mancinis had always considered him family, and no matter what happened between the two of them that would never change. She'd just have to make sure Jax understood he had a family now, one that cared and would be there for him no matter what. Right after she figured out what was going on, and why he hadn't called her himself.

36

JAX

Jax stared at the ceiling, cursing his bad luck. Another few inches to the left and he'd have been home free. Funny how that worked. Still, fifteen stitches wasn't the end of the world. He'd seen worse.

At least no one had been seriously injured in the accident.

Thank God for that.

He'd be riding a desk for a few days, but he'd be back on the job in no time.

Maybe it was time to reconsider his emergency contact. Today had been a close call. He'd just barely stopped the doc from calling Becca, promising one of the guys from the house would take him home when he was discharged. And they would. It's what they did. They were family. But the department didn't let you list another firefighter as next of kin.

It wasn't a problem for most guys. Most guys on the job had plenty of family.

All he had was Becca. And the Mancinis.

Not that he was complaining. It was more than enough. He just didn't want one of them getting the call if something did happen to him.

In retrospect, it had been stupid to list Becca. When he'd put her down, he'd just hoped no one would ever need to make the call. After all, he'd been on the job for eight years without a single incident.

There's a first time for everything.

Dumb fucking luck. That's what this was.

He glared at his gauze wrapped forearm.

There would be no hiding it from Becca. He'd just have to downplay it when he told her. No need to worry her unnecessarily. With her freelance work and the upcoming exhibit, she had more than enough on her plate. She'd been working so hard to keep everything on schedule.

Hell, she was barely sleeping.

The last thing she needed was added stress. Especially when he was fine.

Still, better she hear it directly from him than from the doc.

Closing his eyes, he shifted his weight, doing his best to get comfortable.

They'd hold him a few more hours, but the doc had promised to get him discharged by nightfall. No way in hell was he spending the night in the hospital.

Anderson would bust him out, if need be.

The curtain slid back with a rattle, and when he opened his eyes, Becca stood there, a look of pain carved on her face.

Pain he'd caused.

She rushed to his bedside and grabbed his hand, holding it tight. "Oh my God, Jax. I was so scared. Are you okay? What happened?"

"I'm fine. Don't worry about me." He glanced over her shoulder, finding the room empty. "What are you doing here? I told them not to call you."

Her head shot up, her eyes going narrow. "Excuse me? What do you mean you told them not to call me?"

"It's not a big deal. Just a scratch, really," he said, squeezing her hand. *Dammit.* This was exactly why he hadn't wanted the doc to call her. "I didn't want to worry you."

"You didn't want to worry me?" she asked, her voice climbing an octave. She pressed her lips together, as if tamping down her volatile temper. "You don't get to pick and choose who gets to care about you and when, Jax. I'm your girlfriend, right? And your emergency contact? That means I get to know what's going on with you. When you're hurt, when you're scared, when you're having a bad goddamn day. Not when you say it's okay, but always."

"Hey," he said, reaching up and stroking her cheek. "Why are you getting so upset? Look at me. I'm fine."

"Why am I getting so upset?" She snorted and planted her hands on her hips, dark eyes shining with anger. "For a smart guy, you can be pretty dumb sometimes. You want to know why I'm upset, Jax? I'm upset because I love you. I. Love. You. Do you understand now?" She expelled a shaky breath, a tear sliding down her cheek. "The thought of something happening to you, it...takes my breath away."

She *loved* him?

His heart skipped a beat.

Becca Mancini loved him. It was too good to be true. Especially after everything they'd been through over the years.

Then reality came crashing back down.

She loved him. A man with one of the most dangerous jobs in the city.

Every time he went to work, every time she got a call like this one, she'd be in hell, wondering if he'd be coming home to her again.

How could he expect her to live like that day in and day out? He chose this life; she didn't. Hadn't he caused her enough pain over the years?

He ground his teeth together. How could he have been so thoughtless? He'd never really had to worry about the risks his job posed, because he'd never had to worry about anyone else before.

Only himself.

"Jax? Say something."

"Sit down," he said, scooting over in the bed and making room for her to climb in with him. When she was settled next to him, her sweet scent overpowering the smells of disinfectant and bleach, he took her hand again, giving it a light squeeze. Now wasn't the time to ponder his stupid mistakes, not when she'd just confessed her love for him. No, he owed her so much more than that. "I love you, Becca Mancini. I've known for a while now, but I didn't want to rush you. I think I've always loved you." She beamed up at him with tears in her eyes. Tilting her mouth up to meet his, he placed a gentle kiss on her lips. "I just didn't recognize the feeling for what it was before."

She curled up next to him, burying her face in his shoulder. "Yeah, it can be pretty hard to sort out those love/ hate feels."

"Exactly." He leaned down and kissed her forehead, thankful the day had gone his way.

"For the record," she said, poking him in the chest. "You'd better never scare me like this again. Ever."

His heart sank, spiraling down, down, down.

What she was asking? He couldn't promise her that, no matter how badly he wanted the words to be true.

The job was dangerous. Unpredictable. Potentially lethal.

He'd accepted the risks a long time ago, and he couldn't—wouldn't—lie to her about it.

Refusing to make a promise he wasn't sure he could keep, he pressed his lips together and held her tight.

37

BECCA

BECCA shimmied into the black lace cocktail dress she'd borrowed from Erin, feeling like a kid playing dress up. With three-quarter-length sleeves and a boat neck, the sheath style was classic, understated, and sexy. It was also a far cry from her usual leggings and T-shirts.

Thank God Erin had let her borrow it because, being the clichéd starving artist she was, there was no money in the budget for a new dress.

Especially not a two-hundred-dollar Aidan Mattox cocktail dress she might only wear once.

She turned to the mirror, a swarm of butterflies taking flight in her belly.

The reception started in one hour. She was cutting it close. Too close.

Hell, she was still trying to wrap her mind around the idea that she was going to her first gallery exhibition. It was surreal.

It was also terrifying.

Putting her work out there for others to judge and question and critique? It was *hard*.

Despite the fact that she'd put it on display for public

consumption, her art was incredibly personal. Each photo she'd selected held meaning to her, and while she wanted to tell those stories in her own voice, the prospect of selling her work to strangers made her a little sad, like she was losing a piece of herself. Of course, selling nothing and never booking another exhibition would be even more disheartening.

Shoving her fears aside, she studied her reflection.

At least she looked the part. Great dress, sexy shoes, fancy updo. No small feat considering her hands were shaking so badly she'd had a heck of a time wrestling her hair into submission and pinning it tight.

Her stomach growled, reminding her the only thing she'd managed to choke down all day was a handful of saltine crackers.

Too nervous to eat meant too nervous to drink, so she'd given herself a one-drink limit.

The last thing she wanted to do was get tipsy at her first event.

She glanced at the clock for the eighth time. Apparently Jax was running late, too.

She tried his phone and got voicemail, leaving a short message.

They hadn't spoken since their fight the night before, when the captain had called and asked Jax to cover a shift on his day off. He'd been happy to do it, promising he'd be home in time for her show, but she'd been too stressed about the gallery opening to think straight, and they'd argued about it. She'd asked him if he understood how important the show was to her, and he'd accused her of not understanding the job.

Not *his* job. *The* job.

Still, even if he was mad, he'd never miss her gallery opening. Not after he'd promised to be there.

He was probably just running late.

No big deal. They still had time.

Might as well use it productively. She went to the kitchen and grabbed a few more saltines, forcing herself to nibble on the bland crackers. When she was done, she washed her hands and checked the time again. Then she checked her phone.

Maybe she'd missed his call.

Nothing.

A fine sheen broke out on her forehead. They were going to be late.

Where the hell was he? She tried his phone again—feeling like a stalker—and again got his voicemail.

Shit.

What was she supposed to do? She couldn't wait much longer. It was opening night, and she couldn't be late. They'd never book her again.

He knew how important this night was to her. What could possibly be keeping him?

Only one thing. *The job.*

Her gut clenched. Something was wrong. It had to be.

Do not let your imagination run rampant. Maybe he just got a call. If he was on a call, he would be inaccessible. It didn't mean anything was wrong. *Just leave another message.*

Beep!

"Hey, it's me. I'm not sure where you are, but please call me as soon as you get this message, no matter what. I need to know you're okay." She checked her watch. "I'm heading over to the gallery, but I'll leave your name at the door. I hope you can make it, but if not, just call me, okay? I need to know you're safe. I love you."

She disconnected, her stomach sinking like a lead balloon.

She should've skipped the crackers.

Stop! Stop overreacting. Everything is fine. So he's running late. It happens. It's not that big of a deal.

The last thing he'd want her to do would be to sit around and worry. He'd want her to go and enjoy her night. Make the most of the opportunity and network with other artists and critics.

So that's what she'd do.

Arriving at the gallery with ten minutes to spare, she checked in with the curator and grabbed a glass of wine, reminding herself it was meant to be ornamental.

When the doors opened at six, there was a steady stream of traffic through the gallery.

She greeted her friends and family as they trickled through, making excuses for Jax's absence, which seemed to be top of mind for everyone. Doing her best to quell her nerves—about her art and about Jax—she focused on engaging guests about the pieces hanging on the wall. After all, her job tonight was to help sell the Rebecca Mancini brand and get people talking about her work.

Surprise, surprise. There was a lot of interest in the black and white of Jax.

It had been a last-minute addition, but Madeline had agreed it rounded out the series nicely, adding a new layer of intensity to the collection. Unfortunately, discussing it endlessly did nothing but intensify her anxiety.

By the time nine o'clock rolled around, she couldn't get out the door fast enough.

The reception had gone well by all accounts—or as well as could be expected given her mind was a million miles away—and she felt pretty damn good about her first showing. The early feedback had been positive, not that she had much to compare it to. The real feedback would come in the critic's formal reviews.

The lights were off at Jax's apartment when she arrived. She rang the buzzer anyway. If he wasn't home, she'd sit on his front steps and wait all night for him if she had to.

No answer.

She rang the buzzer again. Just in case.

Still no answer.

Just as she was sitting down to make herself comfortable, his voice came over the intercom. "Yeah?"

She jumped to her feet. "Jax? It's Becca."

The door buzzed, and she let herself in, relief flooding her veins. He was home. And safe.

She raced up the stairs, finding the door to his apartment open.

"Jax?" She scanned the dark living room, taking in the beer bottles that littered the coffee table. He'd been drinking. A lot. Her eyes raked over Jax, who sat on the couch in a pair of track pants and nothing else. His eyes were bloodshot. The five-o'clock shadow on his jaw suggested he hadn't shaved. She'd never seen him like this before. Ever. Something was wrong. Very wrong. She took a tentative step forward. "Is everything okay?"

"Just peachy," he said, taking a pull on his beer. "I'd offer you a drink, but this is the last one."

"Are you drunk?" Stupid question. The answer was pretty damn obvious. "What is going on? Is this about last night? Because I didn't mean to—"

"Just having a beer." He shrugged as if it were no big deal. "Or twelve."

Anger sparked low in her belly. Had he forgotten about their plans? It was only the biggest night of her life.

"I called." *Stay. Calm.* "I was worried about you."

"I shut my phone off." He set his beer on the table, next to the phone. Even in the dim light, she could see the screen was cracked. "I needed some time to think."

"You missed the reception. At the gallery," she clarified, just in case his beer-addled brain couldn't make the connection.

Judging by his current state, it was a pretty safe bet he might need the assist.

He looked up at her, an emotion she couldn't identify flickering in his eyes, and grabbed his beer. When he raised it to his lips and took another pull, her Italian temper exploded, earning her a week's worth of Hail Marys. The scene before her was new, but the feelings it evoked—the sickening, disheartening crash of betrayal, the disappointment, the overwhelming feeling of being inadequate—those felt all too familiar, and it disgusted her.

"Jesus, Jax. Are you fucking kidding me right now? This is the biggest night of my career, and you're sitting here getting shitfaced?" She fisted her hands, nails digging into the soft flesh of her palms. The stabbing pain only fueled her anger. This could not be happening. The man she loved wouldn't do this to her. Not again. "I've been out of my mind with worry, and you couldn't even be bothered to return a goddamn phone call?"

38

JAX

Jax sat quietly as Becca unleashed her temper, keeping his face a blank mask. It wasn't exactly hard after a dozen beers. She had every right to be angry, but he couldn't quite bring himself to feel...*anything*.

Apparently the beer was doing its job. Keeping everything—the guilt, the pain, the anger—at bay.

Dammit, that's what he needed. An escape.

From all of it. If only for the night.

Because every time he closed his eyes, all he could see were the flames. They reached for him, reminding him that no matter how far or how fast he ran, he'd never escape. They'd taken a life last night, and he hadn't been able to stop them.

You're a failure.

He'd failed, and a man had died.

Somewhere in the city a broken family was mourning the loss of a husband, a father, a son. It was his fault, and there was nothing he could do to fix it.

Broken was broken. A fact he knew as well as anyone.

The call had come in at the end of the shift, and it had been a bad one. He'd known it as soon as they'd pulled up. But he'd hoped, hell, he'd prayed—

"Jax?" Becca's voice sliced through his thoughts like a blade. "Are you even listening to me?"

"How could I not?" he asked, forcing himself to do what had to be done. There wasn't enough beer in the world to dull the pain this would bring. "You're screaming loud enough to wake the dead."

"Excuse me?" Her face paled, the color draining from her cheeks.

"Look, I said I was sorry, didn't I?"

"Actually, you didn't," she spat, anger radiating from her. "And this isn't about you missing the show. I understand the job comes first. I get that. I can live with that. But this? You stood me up—*again*—to get drunk on your couch?"

"It's not that big of a deal," he lied, hating himself for hurting her this way. "But if you're just going to keep yelling, there's the door."

She flinched as if he'd slapped her.

Every fiber of his being ached to go to her, to hold her in his arms and apologize, but he had to stay strong. For her. It was going to hurt like hell, but it was better to get it out of the way now, to make a clean break before he did any permanent damage.

She'd be hurt and angry for a while, but she'd get over it. Over him.

His palms began to sweat.

People got over breakups every day. There were other things, far worse things, you could never come back from. He'd always known it in the back of his head, but today it had become clear, when he'd heard her panicky voicemails, begging him to call her back.

That was the tipping point.

He couldn't—*wouldn't*—put her through that.

His father had been destroyed by his mother's death.

By all accounts he'd become an entirely different person, a shell of a man.

He wouldn't do that to Becca. Never to Becca. She deserved so much more. More than a man who was always on call, who missed exhibits and holidays and birthdays. More than a man who could only offer sleepless nights and who might not come home at all one day, leaving her with a flag and a hell of a lot of heartache. She deserved a better life than he could offer.

She deserved a successful photography business.

A doting husband.

Hell, even two point five kids if she wanted them.

The idea of Becca in another man's arms ripped his guts out. But if he truly loved her—and he did, more than life itself—he had to let her go.

No matter how bad it hurt.

"If I walk out that door, I won't be coming back." She leveled him with a glassy-eyed stare, her lips pressed into a firm line. "Do you want me to leave, Jax?"

He glanced at his empty beer. He was going to need another case to get through this night. "I think that would be for the best."

39

———

JAX

JAX AWOKE face down on the bed with the mother of all hangovers.

His skull felt like it was going to split right down the middle. He lifted his head and blinked against the harsh afternoon sun slanting through the open blinds. His eyelids felt like sandpaper, and his mouth was drier than a motherfucker.

What time is it anyway?

He squinted at the clock, trying to decipher the blurry images. Eventually, he abandoned the effort and dropped his head back onto the pillow, cursing himself for drinking so damn much. It was a wonder he hadn't ended up with alcohol poisoning.

Fortunately, he still had some aspirin leftover from his lacerated arm.

If only they weren't in the bathroom.

It was only twenty feet, but it might as well have been a city block.

Deciding to work his way up to movement, he lay still, trying to recount the events of the prior night.

He immediately regretted his decision, recalling the look on Becca's face when he'd told her to leave.

Total devastation. His chest hurt just thinking about it. He'd been a complete asshole.

But it was for the best, wasn't it?

Yes.

He had to believe that or he really would be the biggest prick in the city. He'd just been so angry after the fire call. Losing a life was never easy, whether it was a civilian or a firefighter. Every loss cut close to home.

Every loss left a scar.

They'd been so close, literally within arm's reach of the vic, when the floor had collapsed.

He'd damn near gone with him, but Anderson had pulled him out. Two in, two out. It was their way.

But watching someone fall like that? Knowing you were so close to making the grab?

Knowing one day it could be you?

That shit messed with your head.

There was a reason firemen didn't talk about the horrors they'd seen on the job. It was because they saw the worst of the worst. It was the job. It was his choice.

His burden to bear.

His guilt.

No way in hell was he going to poison Becca with those stories.

Becca.

His gut churned with nausea.

What he'd done, the things he'd said to her...there was no turning back now. It made him sick knowing he'd ruined her special night. It was unforgiveable. He hated himself for it. He could hardly blame her if she hated him, too. That's what he'd wanted, wasn't it?

Enough.

It was time to get up and move on.

He'd make himself fucking crazy if he lay there thinking about her any longer.

Pulling himself to a sitting position, he swung his feet over the side of the bed.

A bolt of pain hit him behind the eyes.

Probably nothing compared to what Becca was feeling. He forced himself to move through his morning routine. It wasn't much, but it was a start.

The first day of the rest of his life.

Because starting over without Becca? It was like starting a newer, shittier chapter where all the things he'd dared to hope for were no longer possible.

He brushed his teeth, took a shower, and popped a few aspirin. They'd done nothing to ease the ache in his chest.

When he returned to his bedroom in search of clean clothes, he stopped in front of the dresser. The pink bear sat on his dresser, looking out of place in the masculine room.

Becca's bear.

The one she'd won.

For him.

Fuck. He missed her already. Missed waking up next to her. Missed the feel of her lips on his. Her laugh. Her smile. The way she quietly watched the world through the lens of the camera. The sassy way she gave as good as she got.

Hell, he even missed her temper, although he'd gotten a healthy dose of it the night before.

Guilt clawed at his gut.

He yanked open the drawers and grabbed a pair of jeans and a T-shirt, pulling them on and ignoring the condemning stare of the stuffed toy.

Becca was too proud to let him see her cry, but he'd seen the look in her eye when she left. He'd been so sure he wouldn't hurt her this time. He'd never imagined that hurting her might be the only way to protect her...from him.

He picked up the bear, squeezing it tight in his hand.

What the hell have I done?

He hurled the bear across the room. It hit the wall with a quiet thud and slid to the floor.

Unable to look himself in the eye, he turned from the mirror and stalked out of the room.

Was this what his life would be from now on? Helping others but keeping no happiness for himself? And really, did he have any right to be angry or sad or whatever the fuck he was feeling when it was his own dumbass fault?

40

BECCA

Becca stared at *The Post*, words like "promising," "inspirational," and "moving" swimming before her eyes. She'd read the critic's write-up on her work half a dozen times, and she still couldn't tell if the review was good or bad. The biggest night of her career, and she couldn't make heads or tails of it.

Talk about a sad state of affairs.

Even sadder was the fact that she'd cried herself to sleep, just like the old days. Definitely not how she'd imagined celebrating her first gallery exhibit. Of course, she hadn't imagined Jax getting shitfaced and breaking up with her, either, so it just went to show how unpredictable life could be.

But it wasn't unpredictable, was it? Hadn't she known all along this would happen? Wasn't this why she had the stupid three-date rule in the first place?

Jax had taught her that lesson at fifteen. And here he was, offering a refresher course ten years later.

Stupid. Stupid. Stupid.

She should've listened to her gut.

Instead, she'd listened to her heart and look where that had landed her. Home alone, nursing a broken heart, and feeling like she'd been dropped in a vat of Jell-O. The whole world was muted. The sights, the sounds, the colors.

Hell, even her movement was sluggish.

A broken heart will do that to you.

And her heart was broken. It was the real deal this time. Shattered into a million tiny shards she couldn't even fathom piecing back together.

It was still too fresh. The pain cut like a knife, leaving her raw and exposed and weak.

God, she was weak, wasn't she? Especially when it came to Jax.

He was a habit she just couldn't kick.

Jax.

Against her better judgment, she'd let him in—again— and now she was paying the price. *Again.*

Only it was worse this time, so much worse.

She *loved* him. And that pain? It was visceral, cutting her down in ways she wouldn't wish on her worst enemy. She'd never felt anything like it. Her heart ached for what she'd lost, what they'd lost.

Even breathing hurt.

Pressing a hand to her mouth, she suppressed a sob, refusing to let another pass her lips no matter how damaged she felt. She'd been so naive, thinking he wouldn't hurt her again. Believing he'd changed.

Fine, maybe he had changed.

Hell, he'd proven it time and again. But in the end, it hadn't mattered.

Maybe they just weren't meant to be. Maybe she was one of those dark, lonely artists destined to suffer for her craft. Because after everything she'd done, after all the changes she made in her own life—changing her name, her appearance, her attitude —she'd landed in the same place.

Broken. Miserable. Alone.

A fresh wave of tears leaked down her cheeks.

How could she be so careless with her heart? She'd known from the start that letting Jax slip past her defenses was a bad idea. She'd even known he was the one man who could eviscerate her, drawing her in with his good looks and charm.

So why had she let him talk her into it?

And breaking her three-date rule? That was just asking for trouble.

Sure their time together had been amazing, some of the best weeks of her life, but in the end, it wasn't enough. It would never be enough.

She would never be enough.

Pulling a tissue from the box in her lap, she wiped her nose.

The way he'd looked at her last night, his eyes flat and uncaring? That wasn't the same man she'd fallen in love with, the man who'd lit a fire in her soul, finding passion she hadn't even known existed. It couldn't be. She refused to believe it.

Not that it mattered, given how he'd stood her up and kicked her out of his apartment all in the span of one night.

She slumped in her chair.

Not her finest hour. Or his.

So what had happened to make him lash out like that?

No. She would not waste any more time making excuses for Jackson Hart. Nor would she waste any more tears on him. She'd found a way to get over him once before, and dammit, she'd do it again.

No matter how difficult and soul-crushing it proved to be.

After all, she was an artist. She'd find a way to channel her pain into her work, and she'd come out the other side better for it. Jax may have broken her heart, but he would not break her.

She was Brooklyn strong. Always had been, always would be.

41

———

JAX

JAX STEPPED through the door to Mancini's feeling like an intruder. Even with Chris's invitation it didn't feel right being there. Not after what he'd done to Becca.

Guilt and shame washed over him, hitting him harder than the blast of cool air the ancient AC was pumping out.

It wasn't fucking right. *He* wasn't fucking right.

He turned to leave.

"Hey, Jax! Get your ass back in here." Chris slung a bar towel over the shoulder of his Yankees jersey. "They're just about to throw out the first pitch."

Resigned to his fate, he joined his friend, taking a seat at the end of the bar where he could watch the big screen in peace.

Chris slid a bottle of lager across the bar.

"Thanks, man."

"Forget about it," Chris replied, eyes glued to the screen.

They watched the top of the first in silence.

The Yankees got a runner on base, but failed to score. Chris hollered at the TV like the hot-blooded New Yorker he was, while Jax nursed his beer silently.

Guilt gnawed at his gut. Why the hell had Chris asked him to stop in anyway?

He glanced around the bar, half expecting to see Becca come prancing out of the kitchen in one of her funky T-shirts. But no, Chris had assured him she wouldn't be there. She was going into Manhattan, which inspired an entirely different flurry of unpleasant emotions.

Was she at Stout tonight, looking for his replacement?

His shoulders slumped. Even if she was, he had no right to feel anything but happy for her.

This was his choice. And he wanted her to be happy. The last thing he wanted was for her to be miserable like him.

Still, the idea of her moving on so quickly hurt like a motherfucker.

When he looked up, Chris was staring at him. Okay, maybe glaring would be a better word for it. Not that he didn't deserve it. He sure as hell did. Frankly, he counted himself lucky his old friend hadn't dragged him into the back alley and beat the piss out of him...yet.

"I should kick your ass, you know."

Jax nodded. What could he say? He'd been thinking the very same thing.

"I haven't seen Frankie like this since she was a kid." Chris braced his arms against the shiny bar. "I don't get it, man. I mean, I'm all for the single life, but if you're both so effing miserable apart, why aren't you together?"

"It's complicated," he muttered, taking a pull on his beer.

The icy lager slid down his throat easily, reminding him of the last time he'd touched alcohol. The last time he'd lost control.

That wouldn't happen again. Not that it mattered.

He had nothing left to lose.

"Complicated?" Chris snorted. "Horses are fucking

complicated. Women ain't that complicated. Why don't you try me? Just leave out the sex stuff, or I really will have to break that pretty nose."

"You wouldn't understand." He looked around the bar, at Mancini's, and realized just how much he envied his friend. "You've got this Brady Bunch life with two parents who love you, and a sister you'd give your left nut to protect, and there's all this love and support and stability. Do you have any idea how lucky you are?" He raked a hand through his hair, hating the vulnerability of his words. "I didn't have any of that growing up. You know what I had? I had an old man who lived at the bottom of a bottle, and a mother I can't even remember."

"Listen, I get it. You were on the shit end of spectrum the day they handed out families." Chris paused. "But what's that got to do with my sister?"

"Everything." Jax pounded his fist on the bar. "Everything. I had a bad night on the job, and all I could think about was Becca. Like, what if it was me who didn't come home, you know? I saw what it did to my dad, and I never want to put Becca through that. Ever." He raised the bottle to his lips. "Better to end things now than risk that kind of hurt."

"For her or for you?" Chris snorted. "New York's Bravest. What a fuckin' joke. I was so proud when I heard you joined the FDNY, but, man, that's some cowardly shit right there. You didn't break things off for her. You did it for yourself. At least have the courage to be honest about it."

He slammed his beer down on the counter, ready to defend the FDNY and himself. But this wasn't about the job, was it?

It was about him. It had always been about him.

His fears. *His* cowardice.

"You want what I got?" Chris asked, not waiting for a reply. "Family means you take the good with the bad. It ain't gonna be sunshine and bunnies every day, but we stick. We take care of each other. That's what family is." Chris wiped up the ring his beer had left behind. "Besides, Frankie's a grown woman. She can take care of herself, and she can sure as shit make her own decisions."

"I know that," he bit out.

She'd told him the same thing on no less than a half dozen occasions.

"Do you? Because from where I'm standing it looks like you're trying to run the show, and it ain't working out so good. For either of you."

Fuck.

Chris was right. Breaking things off with Becca had been stupid and selfish.

He hadn't done it to spare her feelings, he'd done it to protect his own. He'd been so damn scared of causing someone else the kind of pain he'd carried his whole life that he'd pushed away the only woman he'd ever loved.

The one time he'd needed her most, the one time he should have been running to her, he'd run from her.

He wasn't so different from his old man after all, always running the wrong goddamn direction.

The realization hit him like a backdraft, incinerating the cowardice he'd wrapped around himself like a fire blanket.

He'd fucked up big time. Becca probably wouldn't speak to him ever again.

After all, she'd given him a second chance, and he'd blown it, just like she knew he would.

No. No more cowardice.

He would find a way to show Becca the real Jackson Hart. The one who loved her fiercely and would do anything to win back her trust and her heart. If she gave him the chance, he wouldn't just be the man she needed. He'd be the man she deserved.

42

———

BECCA

BECCA PULLED a stack of prints for Erin to review, offering her friend what she hoped was an appreciative smile. Erin wasn't exactly thrilled about their late-night work session, despite the fact that she'd brought dinner and two bottles of wine.

"It's a good thing I like you. I wouldn't skip happy hour with Johnny Football for anyone else," Erin said, tucking her hair behind her ear.

"You don't even like him," she challenged. "Last week you said he was, and I quote, a colossal jackass."

"True. But he has these muscles I can't get enough of," Erin explained, taking the photos and flipping through them. She nodded appreciatively, pulling two out and setting them to the side. "These are really good." She paused and looked up thoughtfully. "You're not going to forget the little people now that you're a fancy pants photographer, are you?"

"Very funny."

"Who's kidding?" Erin quipped, tucking her legs beneath her on the sleek leather couch. "That piece in *The Post* was glowing. I'll be surprised if you don't sell out the exhibit."

"I don't want to get my hopes up," she admitted.

After the blowup with Jax, she was finding it hard to be too optimistic about anything lest she crash and burn again. Frankly, she wouldn't survive another soul-shattering disappointment. But Erin was right. The images for the FDNY piece had turned out better than she'd expected. There was a lot of good material to choose from.

It was just hard to see the images without thinking of Jax.

Hell, everywhere she went, and every photo she took, reminded her of him in some way.

How could she possibly be expected to celebrate her success when her heart was broken beyond repair? Even her photography, which had always provided light during the darkest periods of her life, seemed bereft of anything remotely resembling joy.

She jerked her eyes from the FDNY photos in Erin's hands.

Seeing them was too damn painful, like pouring salt in a gaping wound.

Yep. That was her heart. A giant gaping wound. The kind that would never heal, leaving her permanently damaged beyond repair.

So much for Brooklyn strong.

Erin pulled another photo. "How many pieces have you sold from the exhibit?"

"Two so far." The critic's reviews had been solid, and they'd helped drum up interest in the exhibit, which was amazing. Really, she couldn't be happier about it. It was just...well, there was one piece she was having trouble letting go. She sipped her wine, knowing that if she asked for Erin's advice, she'd get the cold hard truth. "And I've got an offer on a third, but I'm not sure if I'm going to take it."

Erin's brow shot up. "What do you mean you don't know if you're going to take it? Why not?" she asked. "You're an artist with a day job—what's to think about?"

"The buyer wasn't able to make it to the reception, so they're requiring a personal meet and greet at the gallery as part of the sale." It was a bit mysterious, but art collectors tended to be eccentric, so she wasn't really hung up on the terms, especially given they'd offered the asking price. No, it wasn't the circumstances that left her questioning the sale. She chewed her lip, knowing her friend was likely to give her a not so gentle reality check. "The photo they're requesting is...personal."

"Sweetie, unless it's a picture of you doing the deed, you should take the offer." Erin plucked another photo from the stack. "An opportunity like this doesn't come along every day. You're getting your art into more hands. You're earning money you can use to help get your business off the ground. From where I'm sitting, there's no down side. How personal can it be?"

"It's Jax."

"Oh, sweetie." Erin dropped the remaining photos on the couch next to her. "How're you holding up? Really?"

"You want the truth?" she asked, knowing her friend wouldn't have it any other way. "I feel like I'm fifteen again, and I. Hate. It. I want to stay in bed and gorge myself on Chunky Monkey ice cream and never see his stupid face again. But I'll get through it. One day at a time."

"Look, you know I don't believe in love, but I do believe in you. You've got to shake this off," Erin advised. "Screw fireboy. Trust me, this is his loss."

"Spoken like a true friend."

"I'm serious." Erin refilled both their wineglasses. "You are not some lovesick kid from Brooklyn anymore. You're an amazing woman and a kick-ass artist, and everyone can see it except for you." She scrunched her nose. "And maybe Jax. But he doesn't count because he's obviously a dipshit."

Becca laughed, a silly giggle bubbling up from her belly and roaring out of control until she had tears streaming down her face.

Erin wrapped an arm around her shoulders, holding her until the tears subsided.

"I'm not saying this as your friend," Erin said, her voice taking on the hard edge of Back-alley O'Malley. "I'm saying it as someone who believes in your talent. Take the offer."

43

BECCA

BECCA SLIPPED into the gallery just before closing time, wishing she had half of Erin's determination. She'd taken her friend's advice and agreed to sell the photo, but it hadn't been an easy decision. Despite the way things had ended with Jax, or maybe because of it, she wanted to hold onto... *Jax*.

Selling it felt unnatural, like losing a part of her soul that could never be reclaimed.

Unfortunately, Erin was right. Business was business and she needed to make the sale.

That was kind of the point of being an artist.

Squaring her shoulders, she wove her way through the gallery, heading straight for the room where her work was on display. Better to suck it up and get it over with. She just hoped the buyer didn't have too many questions.

The last thing she wanted to do was burst into tears talking about Jax.

Then again, she was a bona fide artist now. Eccentric behavior came with the territory, so maybe they'd consider it a bonus.

The lights were dim when she entered the space, but she

wasn't alone. There was a man studying her work. His back was to her, but it didn't matter. She knew that body as intimately as she knew her own. Standing there in his dress uniform with his hat tucked under his arm, he looked every bit the perfect gentlemen.

Jax.

Her heart stuttered at the sight of him. She'd missed him something fierce this last week. It was hard to believe he'd become such an integral part of her life, as necessary as fresh air and tiramisu, in such a short time. But that time had passed.

So what was he doing at the gallery?

It didn't matter. She couldn't do this right now. She needed to keep her head about her, to talk art with a prospective client.

That would be impossible with Jax in the gallery.

Quiet as a mouse, she backed out of the room.

Madeline would have to reschedule the buyer, tell him she had food poisoning or something. Surely the curator would understand. Besides, a lover's quarrel in the middle of her gallery, even at this late hour, wouldn't be good for business.

He turned, his eyes finding her immediately, as if he'd know she was there all along. "Becca."

She froze. "Jax."

"Please don't leave." He took a tentative step forward, partially closing the gap between them.

Why did he have to make that uniform look so damn good?

"I can't do this right now," she blurted, hating the way her body reacted to the sight of him with hard nipples and damp panties. Stupid hormones. "I'm meeting a prospective buyer."

"I know." He spread his hands and then clasped his hat at center mass. "I requested the private showing. I hope you don't mind."

Mind? She most certainly did mind. After he'd thrown her

out of his apartment and stomped on her heart? What the hell was he playing at?

She drew a calming breath.

No need to get herself kicked out of the gallery for acting like a lunatic.

They were both adults, and she was perfectly capable of telling him where he could stick his private showing without raising her voice.

She stalked across the room, heels clicking on the hardwood floor.

"This is a powerful image," he said, pointing to the photo of him on the ladder. She opened her mouth to give him a piece of her mind, but he cut her off. "I know we have a lot to talk about, but before we get into that, can you talk to me about this photograph? Please?"

She snapped her mouth shut.

Fine. She'd play along, if that's what it took to find out what he was up to.

Just as she had a hundred times before, she studied the image. "The lighting isn't quite right." She tilted her head, a frown tugging at the corners of her mouth. "And I wish I'd gotten a slightly better angle."

"Is that your sales pitch?" The corners of his lips twitched. "If so, it could use some work."

She gave him the side eye, hating that she noticed his stupid dimples. "What do you want to know?"

"I want to know what you see as an artist." He arched his brow, his eyes searching hers as if the answers might be hidden in their depths. "Why did you choose this photograph for your exhibition?"

It was a good question. It wasn't technically perfect, so why had she chosen it?

"When I look at this photograph, I see so much more than a

fireman saving the life of a child. Don't get me wrong, that image is powerful in its own right."

"But that's not why you chose it," he said, finishing her thought. His blue eyes were clear and bright, like summer skies, unlike the last time she'd seen him.

"Your eyes—" She hesitated. "I mean, the subject's eyes convey strength, courage, resilience. The very best of the human spirit." She ran her fingers over the frame, reminding herself to keep it professional. "When I look at this image, I feel hope. For humanity and for my city."

He nodded, placing his hand over hers.

A shiver raced down her spine.

Not this time.

She jerked her hand away, refusing to be sucked in by him again.

He'd had his chance. Two, technically. She didn't have a third in her.

"I'm no expert, but I think maybe you missed something." He narrowed his eyes. And was it her imagination or did his shoulders sag just a bit? "You know what I see when I look at this photograph? Fear and doubt. The subject is afraid. Afraid he won't be good enough, brave enough, strong enough."

"I didn't miss anything," she said, her breath hitching in her throat. "Art is subjective. We each see what we want to see, what speaks to us. The reason this piece is so powerful, the reason people are drawn to it, is because it affects each of us differently. But I have to believe the good outweighs the bad. Every day we make choices that shape who we are as people, and on this day"—she tapped the glass—"courage reigned supreme."

"You always see the best in people, even when they don't see it in themselves." He toyed with his hat, but his eyes remained locked on hers. "Even when they don't deserve it."

"Jax—"

"Please, just hear me out," he said, his words thick with emotion. "I want to apologize to you. For ruining your reception and for every terrible thing I said to you that night. I know how important that day was to you, and dammit, I wanted to be there to share it. I was so proud of you. I still am." He shifted his weight, looking anything but comfortable.

She could relate. Her heart was beating double time.

He looked so sincere, as if their breakup had been as painful for him as it had been for her. But that wasn't possible, was it?

After all, this was what he'd wanted.

He'd told her to leave, knowing she wouldn't come back.

"Really, Jax?" She crossed her arms over her chest. It wasn't much, but it was the only protection she had left. "Because that's not how it felt when you stood me up— *again*. Or when you told me to leave your apartment."

His shoulders fell. "I know. I—"

"No," she said, cutting him off with a jerk of the hand. "You don't know, Jax. You really don't. So why'd you do it? I just...I don't understand. Things were going so well before..."

"Before I fucked it all up?" he finished.

She sighed, rubbing her temples as her emotions spiraled out of control. "Yeah, pretty much."

"The company caught a tough call, and I was in a bad place. We...I...lost a life. I was frustrated and angry, but that's no excuse for what I did or said. I acted like a coward, projecting my fears onto you. I told myself I was protecting you, when in reality I was protecting myself. I listened to those voicemails you left, to the fear in your voice, and I couldn't bear the idea of hurting you...if someday I didn't come home." He paused, drawing a deep breath. "My father, he was never the same after my mother died. His grief destroyed him and, in turn, our family. I couldn't bear the idea of putting you through that, of ruining the amazing person you are, the bright future that lies ahead. I never wanted to hurt you, Becca."

"Let me get this straight," she asked quietly, pulse thundering in her ears. "You thought it was better to hurt me now than risk that kind of future devastation?"

He nodded, the sadness in his eyes overwhelming. "I was an idiot."

"Damn right you were an idiot. You were afraid of hurting me? That's what this was all about?" she asked, throwing her hands up. "You put us both through hell because you were afraid of what *might* happen? Don't you think I get scared, too, sometimes?"

Despite the angry rhetoric, her armor was slipping.

She could feel the fortress she'd built around her heart falling.

In his own misguided way, he'd been trying to do the right thing. And even if she didn't agree with his logic, she could understand why he'd chosen wrong. He'd never risked his heart, and he'd never had anyone willing to risk theirs for him.

Hell, he'd told her himself that he didn't know what love was before...*her*.

He reached out and stroked her cheek, setting fire to her skin. "This thing between us...fuck. Becca, I love you. Always have, always will. And it scares the shit out of me."

Fear was a powerful emotion.

She knew firsthand what it was like to live with it day in and day out, afraid to take a chance.

After all, hadn't she let fear control her life for the last ten years? It wasn't until Jax had come along that she'd let go and—

Wait. Did he just say he still loves me?

44

JAX

JAX WATCHED as Becca processed his words. He could almost see the wheels in her head turning as she decided how to respond to his bumbling apology. It hadn't gone exactly as he'd planned, but that didn't matter. The only thing that mattered now was her answer.

Would she tell him to pound sand? Or would she give him another chance?

Shit.

He didn't deserve another chance, but he wanted it more than he'd ever wanted anything in his life.

He'd do whatever it took to win her back.

"One more chance, Becca." He reached out, touching her arm. "Just give us one more chance. We were so good together. I know we can be good together again. I'll do whatever it takes to prove it to you."

"You don't hurt the people you love," she said, her chest rising and falling heavily. "You don't push them away. Not to protect them and not because you're scared."

"I know I fucked up," he said, prepared to beg if that's what it took to make her understand that losing her would *break* him.

"And you don't knock them down again when they make a mistake." Her chin trembled. "You pick them up, and you dust them off, and you love them, like you always have and always will."

Wait. What was she saying?

"Becca—"

"Shut up and kiss me, Jax."

His ears were playing tricks on him. Did she just say "kiss me?"

That couldn't be right, could it?

One look at her face, at the raised brow that said "what are you waiting for," and he had his answer.

He slipped an arm around her back and pulled her close, enjoying the way she fit perfectly against him, as if she'd been made for him alone. Hell, maybe she had been. That was the beauty of it.

He lowered his mouth to hers, committing the moment to memory and savoring the sweet taste of her lips. His mouth moved over hers slowly, teasing her with a slow build.

"You call that a kiss?" She tangled her fingers in his hair and tilted his head, giving herself better access to his mouth as she spread his lips with her tongue and delved inside.

She kissed him like a woman starved for intimacy, devouring his lips with urgency.

When she finally released him, he was panting, the hard ridge of his erection straining against the fitted dress pants. "Before you say anything else, I need to know if you can forgive me, if you can you give me one more chance to be the man you deserve?"

"Didn't I just say you were forgiven?" She grinned up at him, her face glowing with excitement, her eyes filled with love. "Clearly I've still got a lot to teach you about relationships and loving people."

His heart swelled. "I promise to be a diligent student. Starting right now. Let's get out of here."

"I thought you'd never ask," she whispered, glancing at the door. "My place or yours?"

"Yours. It's closer." He kissed her again, hard and fast this time. "What about my artwork?"

"The gallery has a delivery service."

Ten minutes later they fell through the door to her apartment, tearing off their clothes. They never made it to the bedroom.

He pinned her against the front door, cupping her ass and lifting her in the air as she opened herself to him. They were both primed and ready, and he drove deep into her with the first stroke, seating himself to the hilt.

He groaned, lowering his forehead to hers as her body clenched him tight.

Withdrawing, he slid back into her, watching her as he moved so he could memorize the look on her face and relearn all the places that made her moan with pleasure.

"I missed you, too." She closed her eyes and rocked her hips as he pumped into her, their bodies moving in unison. "My little battery-operated friend has nothing on you."

"Open your eyes, Becca." He stopped moving, and she did as he instructed, looking up at him from beneath heavy eyelids. "From now on, the only one getting between your thighs is me, understand?" He pumped into her and slowly withdrew. "My dick." He gave her another stroke, eliciting a moan. "My mouth." He buried himself deep. "My fingers. That's all you'll ever need."

Nodding, she fused her mouth with his, ravishing his lips as he pushed them both toward climax, their bodies spiraling higher and higher with each crash of their hips.

Just when he was sure he couldn't hold out any longer, she threw her head back, banging it against the door as she called his name, riding out the aftershocks of her orgasm and pulling him over the edge with her.

His body went rigid, sealing itself to the woman he loved as they lost themselves in carnal pleasure.

Afterward, he held her tight, promising himself he'd never let go.

No matter what life threw at them, they'd face it together. Because a life without Becca in it? It wasn't a life worth living, and nothing was going to come between them this time. Not the past, not the job, and definitely not his fears.

With Becca, he was finally home.

EPILOGUE

BECCA

Becca studied her date across the table, wondering how he felt about exhibitionism. No one was paying a bit of attention to them. If she wanted to give it a go, there was no time like the present.

She slid her foot up his calf and between his legs, following the hard muscles of his thighs straight to his cock. Thank God for floor length table linens. Otherwise, she'd be well on her way to getting them both kicked out of the black-tie affair.

Not that it would be the worst thing in the world.

Getting kicked out meant they could go find a bathroom or a coat closet or some other very private place to finish what they'd started.

Okay, technically, what *she'd* started, but that was hardly the point.

Jax's eyes nearly jumped out of his head as she massaged him with her foot, his erection growing thick at her touch. He shifted in his chair, his face turning a deep shade of crimson.

Enjoying the tortured look on his face, and knowing he'd return the favor later, she blew him a kiss.

It was a fancy-pants charity dinner, the kind they both hated, but it was for the FDNY, and as guests of honor, their presence would be missed if they slipped away for a quickie in the bathroom. Especially since they'd soon be announcing the models for a FDNY Hall of Flames special edition calendar.

Jax and his peers had been so popular they'd sold a record number of calendars, prompting a special edition for the New Year, with the most popular firemen of all time. Erin liked to think sales were stimulated by her Bravest series, and maybe they were. The only thing Becca knew for sure was that everywhere they went, women were fawning all over Jax.

Talk about irony.

If someone had told her a year ago that she and Jax were a perfect match, she'd have laughed in their face. *Hard.*

Now? She couldn't imagine her life without him. Or without moments like this one.

She rubbed her foot against his cock, applying more pressure.

He moaned. And then he coughed, raising his napkin to his lips to cover up their bad behavior.

She grinned. Twenty minutes ago, the only thing she could think about was dessert. Unfortunately, dessert was nowhere in sight, and Jax was right across from her, looking far more delectable than any hotel pastry.

A year of hot, sizzling sex and they still couldn't get enough of one another.

The days he spent at the firehouse were long and her bed lonely, but they made up for it when he was home. Now if they could just duck out...

The emcee took the stage, droning on and on about the voting process they'd all engaged in earlier that evening. She continued to work Jax's cock with her foot, knowing there was a real possibility he'd be heading to the stage with the mother of all hard-ons.

He threw his napkin on the table and slipped his hands below, capturing her foot before she could do any serious damage. When his gaze fell on her, there was a wicked gleam in his eye. He began to massage her foot, paying special attention to the arch, which was hella sore from the four-inch stilettos she'd worn against her better judgment.

Crap. If he kept that up, she'd be putty in his hands. Or possibly under the table.

The emcee opened the envelope and began to ceremoniously read the names of the twelve firemen who would grace the pages of the special edition calendar she'd be shooting.

Throughout the room, the men stood when their names were called, acknowledging the applauding crowd as they made their way to the stage. Some waved, some winked, one the younger guys flexed his biceps, drawing a roar of enthusiasm from the women in the room.

"Mr. November: Jackson Hart!"

She jerked her foot free of his grasp, joining the others in their applause.

Much to her relief, Jax was boner-free when he stood and waved to the crowd.

He stepped around the table and lowered his mouth to her ear. "How fitting, since I have so much to be thankful for."

A warm blush filled her cheeks as he brushed his lips across her temple.

She watched with pride as he joined the other men on the stage, the bright lights glinting off his blond hair. It was a stark contrast to the navy uniform that hugged his well-defined muscles as if the freaking thing had been custom made to torture her.

So much for having him all to herself tonight.

Still, she couldn't have been prouder of him, and she was thrilled to be shooting the special edition calendar. She sure as hell didn't want anyone else shooting her man while he strutted around topless.

When all the fanfare died down and Jax returned to the table, he didn't take his seat.

Instead, he reached for her hand, taking it gently in his own. "Ready to get out of here?"

"I thought you'd never ask," she returned, slipping the heels from hell back on her feet. It was going to be a long walk home, but at least she'd be in good company.

When they entered the lobby, he reached into his coat pocket and withdrew a room key. "I booked us a room for the night."

"That sounds like the best idea ever." She didn't have overnight clothes, but who cared? The only thing she needed was the man standing beside her. "I've been dying to get you out of that uniform ever since you put it on."

Jax silently led the way to the elevator bank and ushered her into the first available car.

"You're awfully quiet," she said, wrapping her arms around his waist. A fine sheen of perspiration coated his forehead. Maybe he'd had a little too much of the spotlight tonight. "Contemplating your duties as Mr. November?"

His lips curved, hooking up on the left and revealing the dimple he'd used to get his way more times than she could count.

"Something like that," he said, sliding his hands around her back and pulling her close.

He lowered his face to hers and placed a gentle kiss on her lips, his mouth moving tenderly over hers.

The elevator doors slid open, and he grabbed her hand, leading her down the hall, her heels sinking into the plush carpet with each step. When they reached their room, he paused at the door.

"Close your eyes," he ordered, sliding the card in the lock and withdrawing it.

"Jax."

"If you want me to finish that foot massage, you'd better close your eyes," he warned, sweeping his fingers over her eyes and forcing them shut.

"I don't know what you are up to," she teased, "but don't think I'm going to forget about that foot massage."

"I'd expect nothing less."

He planted a hand on her lower back and steered her into the room. She followed his lead, trusting him implicitly to guide her without letting her stumble over a piece of ill placed furniture. Soft jazz played in the background.

What the hell is he up to?

When they finally stopped, he took her hand.

"Open your eyes, Becca."

She did as he instructed, finding the suite aglow in candlelight and overflowing with red roses. There was an overnight bag on the chair. And, *oh!* Jax was on his knee in front of her, looking up at her with such love, such emotion, she could hardly believe her eyes.

It was like something out of a movie, one of the many she'd watched growing up. Only it wasn't a movie, not this time. This was her life, and the man she adored was on his knee before her.

"Oh my God!" she gasped, bringing her other hand to her mouth. "Jax?"

"Becca Mancini." He reached into his pocket and removed a

tiny box, his eyes glued to hers. "Before you came back into my life, I didn't know the meaning of love or family. You taught me both, helping me understand true love means taking the good days with the bad, and giving your heart to someone you love and trust unconditionally." Her own heart swelled. This was really happening. He opened the box, revealing a brilliant round cut diamond. It was classic, elegant, and perfect. "I don't know how I got so lucky to have you in my life, but I'm sure as hell not going to let you go. Not now, not ever. Marry me, Becca."

The day she'd dreamt of so many times was finally here, and the reality was so much better than any fantasy she'd indulged in growing up. Jax was on his knee asking her to take this leap with him, and she didn't even have to think about it.

He was the only man for her. Always had been, always would be.

The whole moment was surreal, and she wanted to say yes, but she was frozen in time, her brain determined to preserve every last detail of the world's sweetest proposal.

Her silence stretched between them, with Jax's hopeful gaze fixed on her, waiting for her answer.

"I have your mom's tartufo in the fridge…"

"Yes," she gushed, pulling him to his feet, her heart soaring. "Yes. Yes. Yes!"

"Yes to tartufo, or yes to marrying me?" he asked with a crooked grin, relief flooding his eyes.

"Both." She wrapped her hand around his neck and crushed her lips to his, opening herself to him and enjoying the way his tongue skated over her own as he took the kiss deeper, melding their bodies into one.

No woman had ever loved a man as fiercely as she loved Jackson Hart.

She was sure of it.

She loved him so hard she was bursting at the seams, barely

able to contain the emotion stretching her body and spirit in new ways.

Whatever the future held, they'd take it one day at a time. Together they'd build a life and a family, and dammit, she'd get her happily ever after with the sexy fireman whose soul completed her own, and who could ignite her panties with nothing more than a look.

Thank you for reading Seducing the Fireman!
Sign up for Jen's newsletter to receive a FREE book.

www.jenniferbonds.com

ALSO BY JENNIFER BONDS

Waverly Wildcats

Holding Harper

Claiming Carter

Catching Quinn

Scoring Sutton

Protecting Piper

The Harts

Miles and Miles of You

Not Today, Cupid

Royally Engaged

A Royal Disaster

Royal Trouble

A Royal Mistake

The Risky Business Series

Once Upon a Dare

Once Upon a Power Play

Seducing the Fireman

ABOUT THE AUTHOR

Jennifer Bonds writes sizzling contemporary romance with sassy heroines, sexy heroes, and a whole lot of mischief. She's a sucker for enemies-to-lovers stories, laugh-out-loud banter, over-the-top grand gestures, and counts herself lucky to spend her days writing swoonworthy romance thanks to the support of amazing readers like you!

Jen lives in Pennsylvania, where her overactive imagination and weakness for reality TV keep life interesting. She's lucky enough to live with her own real-life hero, two adorable (and sometimes crazy) children, and one rambunctious K9. Loves Buffy, Mexican food, a solid Netflix binge, the Winchester brothers, cupcakes, and all things zombie. Sings off-key.

To connect with Jen, visit www.jenniferbonds.com to sign up for her newsletter and be the first to know about new releases, giveaways, and exclusive content! You can also find her on Facebook, Instagram, and TikTok @jbondswrites.